# Good Fellas
# of the Bible

# Good Fellas of the Bible

*GOD MADE THEM AN OFFER
THEY COULDN'T REFUSE*

*by*

Susan Eaves

Copyright © 2007 by Susan Eaves

Published by Good Fellas Publishing

Printed in the United States of America

ISBN: 978-0-615-21810-6

# Contents

# Dedication

I N loving memory to the three men that profoundly influenced my life and changed me for the better.

To my Dad, I thank you for the street smarts you gave me. I also thank you for the sacrifices you made for my education. You always said you wanted me to have an easier and better life than the one you had. I never understood, until now, what that truly meant.

To my brother, Tommy, I am so appreciative for the generous, wacky, wonderful brother that you were. Thanks for being such a remarkable uncle to my children.

To my beloved firstborn and only son, Clint. Many of your friends called you "Samson" because of your size and incredible strength. I called you son. How grateful I am to God for the twenty-one years He gave you to me. I never knew such a love was possible until you came along.

How I look forward to the day when I will be reunited with the three of you in heaven. Until then, I will work to bring many others with me.

# Acknowledgements

THANK you to my Lord and Savior, Jesus Christ. There are no words to adequately express my gratitude for who you are and what you have done in my life. I pray that many would receive life and hope and a personal knowledge of your love for them through this work.

To my family, I love you and thank God for each of you.

Special thanks to friends who helped make this work possible.

This work became a reality because of many people. To those involved in this project, you have been Jesus with skin on. Thank you for cheering me on with your encouragement, prayers, and ideas. I could not have done it without you.

My pastors Alex and Antoinette Cericola from Healing for the Nations Church in Boynton Beach, Florida, you have been heavenly helpers!

Dennis Eaves, thanks for the title and your special "mob" insights and inspirations.

Genesis Eaves, thanks for allowing Mom to pick your brain with wild ideas late at night.

My fellow editors, Mary Twitty, Elizabeth Mitchell, Pegi Richardson, and Joanne Derstine, your skills, suggestions, and support were priceless. Thanks for your patience and kindness. I know editing Mobspeak and Italian-American slang was an incredible stretch for all of you. I pray that others would come to know your own personal extraordinary writings.

And thanks to prayer warriors, Kathy Faydash, Sharon

and Don Donaldson, Marjory Herfurth, Dee Youngblood, all
the members of Healing for the Nations Church, MaryAnn
D'Angelo, Mary LaVerghetta, Jennifer Busa, Margaret Pace,
Chris Berster, Muriel Wallace, and Theresa Duffy.

# Glossary: Italian-American Slang and Mobspeak Terms*

A made man: official member of the mob inner circle.

*Puttana (Buttana)*: prostitute

*Cappish(Cabbish)*: understand, get it

Cement shoes: another way for saying killed.

Chasing it: term for gambler's high. Rush that comes from gambling.

*Comare*: mistress

*Consigliere*: consultant, counselor for the Mob.

Evil eye: wishing a person ill will.

*Face Contente(Fa che Contente)*: say yes, yes to their face, and then do what you want.

Gangland execution: planned mob killing.

*Cavone(Gavone)*: glutton

Gangster: Mob related

Going Sicilian: to go ballistic, to be crazy, mad.

Good Fella: Someone who operates on the outskirts of the law. May be a member of organized crime but not necessarily.

*Goombas: paesanos*, associates, friends

Hit: contract killing

Iced: "taken out," murdered

Juice Money: forced extra interest

*La Cosa Nostra*: this thing of ours

*La Mana Nera*: Italian for the Black Hand

Made Man: Official member of the inner circle of the Mob.

*Malye*: pig

*Mulyam*: literally eggplant; derogatory term for a black person.

*Ogeda*: stressed, upset stomach, heartburn.

*Omerta*: code of silence.

On the lamb: running from the law

Payback: getting even

Pinched: arrested

Rat: informant

Shadowed: followed

Shake-down artist: squeezes money out of people

Sit-down: mob meeting

Stand up guy: won't testify against his friends, will take the fall for someone else.

*Stunad*: stupid

Taking the Fifth: exercising one's Fifth Amendment rights to not incriminate self.

The big house: the can, prison

The Black Hand: organized crime

Thursday's missing: he's not right in the head

*Umpatz (umbatz)*: crazy

Use Fee: exorbitant interest

Wiseguy: mobster

Under the table: not reported income, untaxed

Whacked: capped, rubbed-out, killed


*All words in the glossary are based on Italian-American slang and Mobspeak from the New York and New Jersey areas. These words are spelled as they sound pronounced, they are **NOT** properly spelled Italian words.

# CHAPTER 1

# The Official Leg-Breaker of Israel

*In Sicily, women are more dangerous than shot guns.*

*-The Godfather*

THIS beast of a man got to break legs for a living, and he loved what he did! His astounding strength and power came from God. As a youth, from time to time, a phenomenal presence would come on Samson. When the presence came, he felt such exhilaration and strength. Sheer ultimate energy pumped through every fiber of his being. When God's Spirit would come upon him he felt invincible.

When he was just a teen, a lion attacked Samson. He tore the lion apart by himself. He told no one what had happened. He could hardly believe it himself. His parents had told him the story of his miraculous birth. But what was this power and ability for? And why had God chosen him?

He was awed by his incredible gift. Samson loved sensing the nearness of God. He knew he wanted to serve this God for the rest of his life. He also knew that his God was more powerful than the god of the Philistines. Just maybe this was his destiny. To defeat the enemy that had oppressed his people for so long. Maybe he wasn't supposed to keep his power a secret any longer.

He started showing his feats of strength to his friends and relatives. He'd uproot ancient oak trees with only his hands. The big brute's bronzed muscles would ripple as he'd pick up things that it would take ten men combined to lift. He tore many wild animals in half with just his bare hands. People started to praise him.

"Samson you're as strong as a god. You're the strongest man in Israel. You may be the one God sent to deliver us from our enemies."

Samson loved the praise. He loved being a giant of a man. The ladies adored the muscular brute. Samson's reputation as the leg-breaker grew. So did his ego.

The presence of God in his life increased, but over time he became cocky and arrogant. He had lots of gorgeous girlfriends who would do *anything* for him. He became intoxicated with this feeling of power. He defeated the Philistines in every battle.

Someone once asked Samson, "Do you believe in healing?" "Healing," he scoffed, "I believe in *hurting*!"

One time a thousand Philistines came out against him, and he cracked every one of their skulls. No one could stand against his fits of rage. His temper was legendary. The men feared and respected him. No one in Israel would dare to oppose him.

He started gambling. He especially loved when he knew he didn't have the money to cover what he had wagered. It gave him an incredible rush to know how close to the edge he was living. He became addicted to power, prostitutes, and gambling.

Samson gambled using riddles. He also gambled by going into rival Philistine territory and spending the night. The leg-breaker was the number one customer of a "secret" Philistine prostitution ring. The Philistines were the number one threat to his nation. Although Samson was well aware of this, he continued his chance-taking ways.

The Philistines knew he spent a night in the home of a harlot. Samson was thrilled that the enemy knew he was there. The Philistines thought they had captured Samson. They closed the city gates. They knew there was no other way out of their city. When this "bad boy" was done toying with them, he got up, lifted the iron city gates off their hinges and carried them up a hill over his head.

The Philistines were furious. Samson had yet another winning gamblers rush! The thrill and excitement of almost getting caught elated him. He continued "chasing it".

Many times, when there wasn't a fight with the Philistines, Samson started one. He enjoyed a good brawl. *Nothing like kicking some butt to make a man feel good!*

Sometimes Samson's conscience would bother him. But when it did he knew just how to handle it. He'd bellow, "Gonna have me some fun tonight. It's skull-cracking time! Gonna break some legs. Gonna find me a hooker or pick a fight with a Philistine pig. And I'm gonna kill 'em *slow.*"

The gambler's parents and relatives tried to warn him about his dangerous lifestyle. After all, he was a Nazarene, set apart by God from his birth. Alcohol was never to touch his lips and a razor was never to touch his head. He observed those two ordinances, but as for the one about having nothing to do with women that were not of his faith—*Well, keeping two out of three commands ain't bad!*

He still had the presence of God in his life. *God appreciates that I keep some of his commands, doesn't he?*

Samson loved being the strongest man in the world. His tanned, buff body bulged through his clothes. His massive chest swelled with pride. *No man can touch me. What a great feeling it is to know that there's not another man alive that can bring me down!*

How right Samson was! It was a woman that would finally bring him down; a woman named Delilah. She didn't need physical strength to defeat him. She had found his weakness. She had such sexy, caring conversations with Samson.

"There isn't anyone that cares about you like me, big boy. You're a remarkable man. No one appreciates your greatness the way I do. How demanding your people are! You have the pressure of a whole nation on your shoulders. Let me massage that tired body of yours. I'm gonna make you forget all your cares. There'll never be another woman who loves you the way I do."

Samson had truly fallen for this woman. She was the Philistines' 'Playgirl of the Year'. Delilah was always there for him and she *never* had a headache. He knew she had been with a countless number of men, but she told him, "Baby, you're the best!"

No man could measure up to Samson. Delilah had always helped ease his guilty conscience. After a long season of plotting with the Philistines, Delilah was accusing him of not caring. She pouted, "All these times I've taken good care of you, haven't I Samson? Don't you care about me at all? Why won't you tell me the secret of your great strength? I've been there for you. You know I won't tell anyone. You say you love me, but you don't show it. You are deceiving me. Shouldn't lovers as close as us share each others secrets?"

Delilah cried and carried on until one day she finally wore Samson out. For twenty years Samson had kept the enemies of Israel defeated. He kept them defeated by keeping his vow to God. He had vowed to never disclose the secret of his great power. After years of compromise and living life on the edge he gave in. He gave up his nations' security secrets to a prostitute.

"My hair has never been cut. My great strength lies in my Nazarene vow to never take a razor to my head."

Delilah wooed Samson to sleep with her caressing touch and feminine charms. Being the resourceful woman that she was, she quickly cut and shaved off Samson's hair. Then she cried out, "Samson the Philistines are coming."

He jumped up to throw them off just like he had done hundreds of times before. But this time it didn't work. The Spirit of God had left him and Samson hadn't even known it.

He had gambled for two decades and always won. He had always loved chasing it. This time he gambled with the anointing of God on his life and lost.

Delilah never even turned around to see what would happen to the man she swore she'd love for all time. With a sigh of indignation she fumed to herself. *Look at the sacrifices I've made for this country. The soldiers should've been more careful. They ruined a perfectly good manicure. I just had my nails done. Not to worry. I'll have them done again, on the way to meet with my financial planner. A girl can't be too careful how she invests her hard-earned money!*

Samson didn't get to see the callous way his mistress left. The Philistines poked his eyes out. They beat him unmercifully. The empty sockets now burned with pain beyond description. His body throbbed from the constant abuse it now received.

But the worst beating he received was the one he gave himself on a daily basis. His self-condemning thoughts were more ruthless than the battering of the Philistines.

*I've played the fool and lost. Why have I been such a jackass? Hadn't my folks tried to warn me about Philistine women? Hadn't God himself tried to warn me by the conscience I always sought to shut out? What made me think that I had something to do with the amazing gift God had given me? Oh, what an idiot I've been! I forgot that everything good I've ever had came from God. Why didn't I listen to Him?*

Eventually Samson stopped beating himself up on the inside. He started to pray again. He listened for the still small voice of God. He cried out to God to use him just one more time.

No one noticed Samson's hair growing.

His faith was also growing. The heart that had been so full

of pride and every evil desire was truly sorry. God heard the cry of his heart.

The Philistines took great delight in displaying their cruelty. They beat him like an animal before the entire country. The sadistic nation of people cheered as they watched the torture. God looked down upon the fallen giant of a man and had mercy. He gave the fallen leader back his strength.

Samson asked the young boy assigned to him to lead him between the two pillars that held up the stadium. The little boy did so. Samson pushed with all his might against both pillars and the stadium collapsed. He killed more Philistines in that single display of strength than he had killed in the previous twenty years.

Samson died that day along with a bunch of Philistines. They went to their reward and Samson went to his. His body was dead, but his spirit man lived on in heaven: forgiven and healed.

*When wisdom enters your heart, and knowledge is pleasant to your soul, discretion will preserve you; understanding will keep you... To deliver you from the immoral woman, from the seductress who flatters with her words, who forsakes the companion of her youth, and forgets the covenant of her God. For her house leads down to death, and her paths to the dead.*

*-Proverbs 2:10-11, 16-18*

For more info about your favorite leg-breaker see Judges 14-16.

# Chapter 2

# The Cop-Killer Who Did Forty Years Hard Time

*"On my command, unleash hell."*

*-The Gladiator*

FROM infancy he was considered royalty. Moses was raised in the palace as a prince. He was a highly-skilled fighter, accustomed to being waited on for every whim and desire. He ate the finest foods and had a vacation home on the Nile River. No one suspected that he would one day grow up to be a high profile, hunted fugitive.

He had two women in his life he called mother. His birth mother, Jochebed, was a Hebrew slave. The woman who adopted him was a royal princess. Jochebed imparted great wisdom and knowledge to him. His earliest memories of her were fond recollections of the countless conversations they had together.

"Moses you are a boy with a purpose. Your destiny is to free your own people, the Jews, from the wicked slave drivers who rule over them. It's a miracle that you are alive. When you were born the pharaoh ordered all Jewish males to be killed by the midwives. But they resisted the pharaoh's orders risking death to save all the newborn boys they delivered. Unfortunately, as those infants grew the Egyptians would come and murder them anyway."

Moses sat on his mother's lap, enthralled with her every word. His chubby, tiny hands caressed his mom's face as she spoke.

"There was great celebration at your birth. Your father and I hid you as long as possible. We knew it was only a matter of time before our oppressors would find out and kill you also. Your sister Miriam and brother, Aaron, prayed with us and asked God to save you. The Almighty One gave us a plan."

"I felt that I was to put you in a basket and take you to the river where I knew the Princess bathed everyday. I requested that God would give you favor and pity in her eyes."

Moses big brown eyes became even bigger as she spoke.

"Were there crocodiles in the river by my baby basket? What about the snakes that bite people? What would you have done if one of them tried to eat me?"

Jochebed smiled as her inventive son played with her hair.

"God protected you from all harm and answered our family's prayers. I put you in the river and left you there with Miriam watching close by. To hear you crying and walk away made me want to die. It was the hardest thing I've ever done."

"What happened next?" Little Moses asked, although he'd heard the story many times before. He cuddled close to his mother as she finished telling him his favorite story.

"You were crying and the princess felt sorry for you. She scooped you up in her arms. The pharaoh's daughter loved you the minute she held you. I had heard that she was childless. A friend of mine worked in the palace as a maiden to the princess. She told me the princess was a kind woman that desperately wanted a child of her own. She and her husband never did have a baby, but when she saw you she said, "The gods have answered my petitions!"

She took you as her own that day. Your sister quickly ran and volunteered a wet nurse. The princess immediately accepted her help. She proclaimed, "It is another sign from the gods!"

"She paid me to take care of my own son. The one true God is a miracle worker."

Moses was a sharp kid and kept his mom's secret. In his infancy and toddler years, he was actually raised in his own home. His father Amram had a heavy workload and suffered at the cruelty of the Egyptian task masters. As he grew beyond the toddler years, he was raised in the palace. The daughter of pharaoh kept his birth mother on as a caretaker for Moses. The princess was unaware that the woman who cared for Moses was his actual birth mother.

As a young boy he thought about the hard life his Jewish father and the other Israelites had. It infuriated him to think about the Egyptian guards mistreating the people that he quietly loved. The Hebrew young man contemplated his difficult situation.

*I am a prince, but all the members of my family are slaves. They are despised and badly treated, and there's nothing I can do to help them. I'm powerless, but one day. . . .*

His silent rage and suppressed secrets caused him to be a stutterer. His royal cousins that he was raised with teased him about his speech impediment causing his halting speech to worsen. Moses was obedient to his royal mom and quick to learn. He was her only child, and she could not have loved him more than if she had actually given birth to him. She had put her own life in jeopardy to represent a Jewish baby boy as her natural born son.

Pharaoh's daughter also had a profound influence upon the young man. She taught Moses that he came from a royal line. He was especially selected by the many gods of Egypt to become more advanced physically and intellectually. He was superior to all of Egypt, but especially the slaves.

She told him, "I drew you out of the Nile, but it was gods

that sent you. All Israelites are your inferiors. The gods have mixed their godlike nature with specially selected humans and made them royalty. If the humans rule their subordinates and slaves well they can also become gods in the afterlife. The only one superior to you, Moses is the pharaoh."

Inside the young man was conflicted. He had power but couldn't use it.

*Which am I: a Jew or royalty? I despise the Egyptians, but my adoptive mom is an Egyptian and she is so good to me. She says the gods have hand selected me to become a ruler of the inferior humans. My Hebrew mom is a slave and tells me I'm the deliverer of my people. Which is it?*

As the grandson of Pharaoh grew, so did his temper. When he would see one of the palace cops mistreating and whipping a Jew, he would imagine taking the whip himself and beating the guards with it.

*One day it's gonna be payback for these degenerates. Just wait 'til I have all the power. Won't they be surprised at what I do to them?*

The day of reckoning finally came. Moses had become a strong, fit young guy. He revealed his true identity to the princess. She always knew he was Jewish, but she was shocked to know he was personally acquainted with his relatives. His royal mom was also concerned about his explosive temper. She cautioned him that the pharaoh would never allow the Egyptian guardsmen to be dishonored. Pharaoh considered his protectors to be an extension of his own authority. He was an arrogant, harsh man.

Moses appeased the princess but was waiting for an opportunity to deliver his people. One day as he was out on palace business inspecting the pyramids, he saw an Egyptian soldier whipping an overworked, underfed Jew. After years of thinking about revenge, it finally happened. He'd suppressed his thoughts of getting even long enough.

Moses snapped and flew into a white heat as his fury erupted at the task master. "You r-r-rotten p-p-piece of d-d-dirt. L-l-let that s-s-slave go, it's-s-s not your right t-t-to abuse him."

The slave driver mocked his stuttering and challenged him. "Come on, Mr. S-S-Sissy pants, I don't have t-t-to listen to you. The Pharaoh's my boss, not his wimpy little grandson. Your grandfather ain't no Jew lover. He'll back however I treat the slaves."

As the task master put his fists up to fight, Moses snapped.

*Go ahead punk, make my day,* thought the raging royal. All the years of pent-up suppressed anger caused him to explode. His strength, fury, and fighting skills were no match for the task master. He beat the man for all the abuse he had witnessed. He bashed his head in thinking about the cruel way his own father was treated. He kicked and punched him for all the rotten things the Egyptians had done to the Jews. He beat him until he realized he wasn't breathing anymore. The slave driver had stopped breathing for several minutes before Moses even realized he was dead.

Moses looked around for any palace cops. They were all out of sight. Moses quickly buried the man. He congratulated himself.

*I disposed of the body so nicely. That will be the last time he mistreats my people. Now we'll see who has the power.*

The next day, he went to the site again to see if any more mistreatment was going on. He saw two Jews arguing. They were pummeling each other. The royal prince went to intervene, but one of the Jews shouted at him.

"I saw what you did to the guard, you cop killer. You talkin' to me about my fists? In fact, right now one of the slave stool pigeons is on his way to rat you out to Pharaoh. Grandpa will pay him big bucks for that information. The enforcers are going to punish ya bad. Now we'll see how tough you are."

Moses was placed on Egypt's ten-most-wanted list. He gave a hasty goodbye to his Jewish mother and fled into the desert to a place called Midian.

He found an oasis with a well. There he came upon yet

another struggle. This time it was several females looking to water their father's flock of animals. Stronger male shepherds were driving them away. Once again the royal hot-head got involved. The highly-trained fighter put the opposition to shame. The father of the female flock herders, Reuel, rewarded Moses. He gave him his eldest daughter to wed.

It was difficult to go from the height of wealth and extravagance, to the wilderness with no luxuries. Inwardly he felt as barren as the desert sands. But he made the best of a tough situation.

Moses spent many lonely days and nights thinking about how badly he had blown it.

*Why couldn't I control my temper? Both of my moms warned me about my rage. I am on Egypt's ten-most-wanted list. I murdered a man. I can never go back. I'll never see my family again. I was supposed to be the deliverer of the Jews, but I'm banned and condemned to this desolate desert. What is left of my life?*

Moses spent the next forty years doing hard time. His marriage was not a happy one. Because of the gloom over his depressing circumstances, he was not an easy man to live with. His wife never understood what it meant to be a covenant Jew. He never tried to contact his Hebrew family. His shame far outweighed his longing to see them. He had also stopped praying to the God of the Israelites. *What would God want with me now? What a failure and loser I am. I've spent forty years just doing time. I've achieved nothing.*

Moses thought God could no longer use him. God thought differently. Moses left Egypt in a day, but it took forty years to remove the prideful, self-indulgent Egyptian lifestyle from the former prince. It wasn't a waste. God was doing a mighty work. He was building a shepherd into a spiritual warrior. Thankfully, God did not look at Moses' past to determine his future.

Moses stopped listening to his accusing, condemning thoughts. He saw the beauty around him though he was surrounded by barrenness. He gradually, ever so slowly, learned that his faith was more powerful than his failures. God, his God, was greater than his mistakes. His spiritual drought had ended.

At the appointed time, God visited him. He displayed his power to the former prince as a burning bush in the desert. Moses turned toward a presence he once knew as a young boy. God spoke to him.

"Remove your sandals, for the place you are standing on is holy ground. I am the God of your father-the God of Abraham, Isaac and Jacob."

Moses hid his face, afraid to look upon God. The cop-killer was shocked to hear the Lord say, "I have seen the oppression of My people who are in Egypt. I have heard their cry because of the wicked taskmasters over them. I know their sorrows. Now I will use you to deliver them."

Moses could hardly speak. "Who am I that I should go to Ph-Ph-Pharaoh and bring out the children of Israel? Who s-s-shall I say has s-s-sent me?"

God said to Moses, "Say to the children of Israel, I AM has sent me."

Moses replied, "But s-s-suppose they will not b-b-believe me or l-l-listen to my voice?"

The Lord said to him, "What is in your hand?"

He responded, "A rod."

The Almighty commanded, "Cast it to the ground."

It became a venomous snake that Moses fled from.

Then the Lord directed Moses, "Reach out your hand and take it by the tail."

Forty years doing hard time had made him better, not bitter. Moses did as instructed. The snake became a rod again as Moses reached out his hand and caught it. God superseded earth's natural laws for his own divine purposes and plans. Moses did eventually become divorced and married another woman of a different race. The bi-racial marriage was also a marriage of two individuals who were united in their faith and belief in the God of the Israelites.

Although Moses had been trained as an expert warrior and developed strong survival skills in the desert, God did not use those abilities to bring down an arrogant, egotistical Egyptian ruler. The covenant-keeping God used a simple rod in the hands of a humble servant to become a powerful weapon. It would overthrow one of the greatest empires of the ancient world.

Through that simple rod Moses would bring ten plagues on the nation of Egypt while protecting the nation of Israel in the same land, at the very same time. Moses would use the rod to part the Red Sea in half and permit the covenant people to escape. They ran from their oppressors, through the middle of the Red Sea, on dry ground. When their enemies tried to follow, the rod that brought the Jews deliverance brought the Egyptians judgment. Every one of their pursuers drowned in the water that day.

The voice of the accuser could no longer find place in Moses. He knew his worth didn't come from his blue blood upbringing, or even his birth parents. What caused him to know that he was valuable was his relationship and covenant with the one, true God. The Almighty turned a former basket-case into a conquering, extraordinary leader.

Because of Moses' miraculous transformation, he was mightily used by God to perform many miracles. In spite of all his shortcomings, he was the author of the first five books of the Bible and the book of Job. He also received the Ten Commandments written on tablets of stone by the finger of God. The Ten Commandments has served as the moral foundation of contemporary leading nations throughout the world.

Moses' critics viewed him as a criminal. They saw him as a divorced, murderer with serious anger management issues, who did forty years hard time. God looked past his faults to see the amazing man he would become.

*Since then, no prophet has risen in Israel like Moses, whom the Lord knew face to face, who did all those miraculous signs and wonders the Lord sent him to do in Egypt-to Pharaoh and to all his officials and to his whole land. For no one has ever shown the mighty power of the awesome deeds that Moses did in the sight of Israel.*

*-Deuteronomy 34:12*

# CHAPTER 3

# Israel's Lethal Weapon

*"Who are you?"*

*"I'm your worst nightmare!"*

*-Rambo*

HE was a keeper of sheep. He also took care of lambs. But this shepherd was no ordinary flock-keeper. As a teenager, he was solely responsible for his large family's provision. He had seven older brothers, however, none of them could help him with the enormous herd. His country was at war. His family was serving in the military and his elderly father, Jesse was unable to help.

His real name was David. His older siblings loved to torment him with the nickname "Lambo". With a house full of brothers, he had to learn how to defend himself early on. His red hair matched his temper.

"I'm gonna kill you." He would scream at one brother as he struggled to get free, while another held him down and sucker punched him. He knew how to throw a good left hook, and then follow up with a right cross to smash the ribs. Just to stay alive in Jesse's home meant fighting for his life on a daily basis. As the littlest, he was often treated as a nuisance. It caused him to be an overachiever.

While his brothers were out with the Israeli troops, David was learning some serious fighting skills. He learned how to battle wild animals that would attack him or the flock. A mountain lion leapt on one of the sheep. Little Lambo pounced on it. He smashed it with a large rock and knocked it unconscious. His well-built arms broke the creature's neck. With his shepherd's rod he beat off a bear trying to tear up the flock.

Young David also learned to become a master with his sling-shot. When the teasing from his older siblings became too much he would threaten them.

He'd scream, "I'm gonna knock you out with my slinger."

The teenager wouldn't miss hitting one of his many older tormentors with some small stones. The slingshot also helped him keep his father's sheep safe from other predators.

From time to time his father would send him with supplies to feed his brothers and other military men. One day as David was feeding the troops, he heard a roar echoing across the valley on the opposite mountain. It was the voice of Goliath, one of the giants in the Philistine military. The armies were at a stale-mate. For forty days, he hurled his intimidations. The giant's continual barrage of words caused every man in Israel to fear.

"Get over here you little sissies. I'll bust you up. I'm gonna kill all you men. Then when I'm done with you, I'll kill your sons, slow. When I finish with them, I'll take your daughters and wives to be my slaves, and I'm gonna have a great time having my way with them. None of you can touch me. You don't have one guy man enough to face me."

Goliath was the champion of the Philistines. His people were barbaric. The uncivilized nation was like a swarm of locusts devouring and destroying everything they came in contact with.

Jesse's youngest became boiling mad when he heard the threats.

"This low-life scum is coming against God and our country.

What are you, a bunch of girls? Do you got nothing left inside? Do something!"

David's siblings got enraged at their baby brother.

"Listen little Lambo, this is a man's war. You're a punk kid. Who did you leave that small group of sheep with? Baa-baa. Can't you hear the lambs crying for their shepherd? This army needs warriors, not puny pests like you. Go back to your flock and that stupid harp. We don't need any more trouble than we already got."

David shot back, "I ain't afraid of him. I've brought every one of you down with my sling shot. I'm gonna drop him like a bad habit. I'll knock him into next week."

A soldier unrelated to the family heard David and brought him to the king. "This kid either has nerves of steel or he's stone cold nuts. But, he is the first one to volunteer."

King Saul was the biggest man in Israel. He knew because of his size, every one expected him to step up and fight this giant. The problem was Saul kept losing the contents of his intestines.

*I can't fight this guy and win. Why did God pick me as the king? Didn't he know this giant was gonna annihilate me? Is this the best God can do?*

"David, you're so young. What makes you think you can kill this giant, when all the fighting military men have been unable to defeat him?"

David rapidly responded. "Your servant was keeping his father's flock. A lion attacked the herd, I knocked him out with a rock and broke his neck. A bear came after the sheep and I beat the living daylights out of him with my staff. God is on my side. Who does this uncircumcised Philistine think he is, defying the armies of the living God?"

*I can't believe the only one we have is a teenager, but I'm not gonna fight this monster. We're gonna lose. At least I'll make it look good.*

"You got guts, kid. I'll send with my personal armor."

*Thank God it's not me going. I'll just put spin on it and tell the people God needs me away from the front lines, I'm the leader. I have to formulate military plans. They'll buy it.*

As David arrived at the battle, he heard the roars.

"Don't you have any real men in that army? Send a warrior who is not a wimp. Let the fight be just between me and him. If he beats me, my people will be your servants. If I win, you Jews will belong to me. Get your sorry selves one soldier who isn't shaking in his sandals."

David kept rehearsing the victories that had brought him to this point. At times when he swore he was going to kill one of his brothers, God would instruct him.

"Peace, be still. Pick up your harp, David. Everything will be okay. It won't always be this way."

At times when the young man felt so lonely he wanted to die, he would pluck his harp strings and feel God's peace. The rage would depart. He would experience contentment and great pleasure in the midst of very difficult circumstances. Jesse's youngest came to know the Lord as his Shepherd. He didn't have to fear or want. The young musician played out his frustrations. David's beautiful melodies would calm his own spirit and that of the animals. Unknown to him, the harpist's music would resonate throughout the countryside. The surrounding neighbors looked forward to his nightly concerts.

The music came from a place of perfect harmony and joy. It came from heaven. It soothed the weary souls of a people at war. Lambo's magnificent voice would sing words of comfort and courage. He thought the songs were just for him, but the God of Israel saw far into the future.

The Great Shepherd inspired David to write his songs down. The music would bring strength to generation after generation of Jews. It would also span time to bring comfort across the ages to the overwhelmed and heartbroken. They would bring calmness to those yet to be born, who would also find themselves at war.

The lyrics, better known as psalms, would never die because God had breathed His own life and power into them. He knew as the end would draw near His people would need faith and reassurance more than ever.

Jessie's lastborn never understood why his brothers took such enjoyment from harassing him. His father never seemed to notice the child of his old age. But God was noticing. He was helping David to become stronger physically and spiritually. The young man would face much tougher battles in the future. His simple experiences would equip him to become a military genius and qualified leader of an entire nation.

When David first started shepherding it seemed to him that his life was destined to be an existence of boring insignificance. Lambo had always been the underdog. The Almighty gave his life meaning and a promise of a future.

The band of Jesse's sons was a giant he'd faced repeatedly. The musician had held his own when greatly outnumbered. It caused him to become a sharpshooter with his slingshot.

It was only by God's strength that he hadn't killed one of them in their sleep. Feeling rejected and irrelevant was another giant he had confronted. During David's times of shepherding, the Lord was watching him in the little things. His faithfulness was pleasing to God. The Great Shepherd changed the flock keeper's way of thinking.

It was Lambo, his Creator and the animals at night under the stars. The Lord would help him to anticipate an attack of a wild animal. "Have your staff ready, a wild dog will attack on the West side."

God even warned him when one or more of his brothers were going to strike him with some sibling stunt. "Three of your brothers will be down by the water waiting for you. Take the flock to the stream on the other side of Bethlehem."

Jesse's littlest would sense a storm was about to hit, even though there was not a cloud in the sky. Later on many times he would know a tempest of adversity was coming when all appeared to be well.

David would follow the impressions being given to him. The Great Shepherd was leading him beside the still waters, while others were laying in wait to harm him.

King Saul had sent him with his own sword and personal armor. Lambo did not bring it on to the battlefield. He had never used these. Instead, he chose to use what he and his Shepherd and had proven over the years. He went down to a brook and picked five smooth stones. He had his slingshot. David finally realized that this was the moment God had prepared him for all of his life.

David boldly stepped on the battlefield.

"What took you so long?" The massive, Philistine pit bull snarled. He was a tower of gargantuan, intimidating strength. He was frightening to everyone but David. Lambo was not moved by the giant's threats or physical appearance.

The young warrior was the first man in Israel to answer him. He ran toward the huge terrorist. The Philistine terrorist did not know the Lord of the Armies was running with Lambo.

David growled back, "Hey ugly, I'll take you up on your great offer."

Goliath hated him the minute he saw him.

"I can't believe they sent me a kid. Let's go, Jew boy."

The giant cursed him by all the gods of the Philistines.

David shouted back, "Yes, I am a Jew and proud of it. Beast be still. I'm gonna hit ya with so many lefts you'll be begging for a right. I'm gonna knock you straight into hell where you belong. I'm not fighting you in my strength. I'm coming at you in the name of the Lord of Heaven's armies. Today God will deliver you into my hands. I'm gonna chop your head off. Your people and mine will know that I didn't win this battle with a sword or spear. The fight isn't mine, it's the Lord's. Right now he's gonna turn you over to me."

As Goliath approached him, Lambo increased his speed to meet him. He got his slingshot out. The sharpshooter aimed for the Philistine's forehead, the one place that wasn't protected. The stone penetrated deeply into his temple.

Goliath didn't realize that it wasn't only Israel he was coming against. He was defying the living God. He didn't have a covenant with the Lord. David did and he had proven the Almighty many times before. Goliath had taken one too many hits to the head and was now out cold. David quickly grabbed the giant's sword and chopped off his head just like he said he would before the battle ever began.

> *The Lord is my light and my salvation; whom shall I fear? The Lord is the strength of my life; of whom shall I be afraid? When the wicked came against me to eat up my flesh, my enemies and foes, they stumbled and fell. Though an army may encamp against me, my heart shall not fear: Though war may rise against me, in this I will be confident . . .*
> *-Psalm 27:1-3*

# CHAPTER 4

# The Crazy King Who Needed to Be Whacked

*"God must love crazy people. He makes so many of them."*

*-Rambo*

THE tall, dark sociopath was stone, cold nuts. He was also King of Israel. The general of the Israelites, Saul was tormented by his own demons. A teenager named David had been hired to play the harp for the mad ruler. For awhile the young harpist's music soothed the king's tortured soul. The royal ruler gave little personal attention to the boy, nicknamed Lambo, as he poured out the beauty of his own spirit. He played in the background a distance from the king.

His highness didn't directly acknowledge him. The king always insisted on darkness when the evil spirits harassed him. David was used to difficult circumstances and people, so the situation did not stress him. He was well acquainted with playing in the dark. When he played the darkness was replaced by light, peace came in place of oppression. The ruler improved so greatly under the boy's music therapy that he told him, "Kid, I appreciate what you've done for me. I'm better now. You can go back home to your family."

Awhile later he was brought before the king again. This time it was because he volunteered to fight the monster, Goliath, the champion of the Philistine army. Even then, the head of Israel didn't make the connection between the boy named Lambo and the one they called David.

After the youngster defeated the Philistine Pit Bull, he went back to keeping sheep. But war broke out against Israel again and King Saul requested Lambo to be brought back down and become a military leader in the Israeli army. The head of Israel was thrilled to have such a brilliant, bold guy in charge.

*Imagine the teenager who relaxed me so much with his moving melodies, is also a little warrior. I wish I had known sooner, it would have made my life made so much easier by using him. The people love the new captain. The men will honor and respect him.*

The king's son Jonathan was about the same age as David and the two became best friends. Although he was a prince, he walked with an unassuming nature and integrity.

One day as King Saul was leading a victory parade, he heard the people chanting, "Saul has killed his thousands, but David has killed his tens of thousands."

It enraged Saul. "Don't the people know that I gave them the victory? I had to be back at the palace making the brilliant military strategies. Who do they think was responsible for winning the war? I saw the raw talent and developed it. David would be nothing without me. He'd still be some scrawny, insignificant shepherd if it weren't for me giving him the opportunity of a lifetime."

The egomaniac continued his ranting. "This is the way he thanks me, by trying to turn my own people against me? This shepherd is a little back-stabbing opportunist. I'll fix him. But I'll have to be careful how I do it. The people adore this little punk."

From that time on the king gave David the "evil eye." Mr. Dark and Deadly consulted with his trusted military advisors. They were really yes men, but the royal ruler had elevated them to their positions because of how they appreciated and recognized his true genius. They helped him concoct a scheme that would take Lambo out, but make the king come out looking as innocent as a newborn.

Saul commanded his servants, "Communicate with David secretly. Tell him I admire and approve of him. Inform him that I want him to be my son-in-law."

The leader's advisors did as he commanded. But Jessie's youngest told them, "I am a poor shepherd and have very little social standing. Who am I that I should be worthy of such an honor?"

The consultants came back to his Royal Craziness with David's reply.

*I underestimated my enemy. This shepherd is so slick.*

"Convey to him that I don't want any payment for my daughter to become his bride. I only want revenge on the adversaries of Israel. If he brings me back the foreskins of one hundred Philistines he can have my girl."

*Mr. Slickster is gonna get annihilated and even God can't pin it on me. I'll be the one the people adore. What a mastermind I am.*

Lambo's close relationship and experiences with the Great Shepherd had given him great insight. He asked God to help him do all that was required. God helped him plan an outstanding military maneuver against the Philistines. Additionally, the Lord of the Armies of Israel gave him favor wherever he went. David brought the king back double what he asked for.

When David returned unharmed and victorious, Saul added paranoia to the list of his growing problems.

*God prefers him over me. Instead of him getting killed, he's getting promoted. He's gonna try to overthrow my kingdom. Treachery is all around me.*

Saul's demons returned with a vengeance. The king was wildly ranting so David was called forth to soothe the savage beast in his boss. Even David's heavenly music no longer helped.

"I hate you, you little back-stabbing jerk!" The leader screamed as flung his spear at the harpist's heart. David narrowly escaped death while the servants and his son, Jonathan restrained the Royal Mad Man.

Jonathan tried to reason with his insane father.

"Father, why are you trying to hurt a man who has only performed good deeds toward you? He has taken his own life in his hands to protect you. Through this warrior the Lord has brought great deliverance to our nation. Why sin against an innocent man?"

Saul changed his mind, but not for long. The Philistines struck Israel again, and David was sent out as a general to handle the garrison operations. He struck the adversaries a mighty blow and returned to his Royal Highness with another enormous triumph.

Once again darkness and light contended for control of the people and the palace. David walked with humility and wisdom before all of Israel and Saul. The king could no longer control his jealousy. In an unprovoked tantrum, the Royal Whacko tried to kill his son-in-law. Lambo's quick reflexes helped him to escape certain death.

Later on, David's wife, Michal, came to warn him of her father's plans for the next morning. He fled that night. The courageous young man couldn't understand why he was being targeted by his king. He recalled a day long ago when he was summoned by his father, Jesse, and the prophet Samuel. He revealed to David in front of his family,

"You are the one God has chosen. He has anointed you to be the next king of Israel. From now on the presence of the Almighty will give you potent power and perception. But see to it that no one hears of this until the time God has appointed for it to come to pass."

David stammered, "But why me? We have a king. Didn't God choose him as ruler of our country?"

"Yes, Saul was once called by God. He has now been rejected because he continually disregarded what God told him to do. He was a people-pleaser and feared the Israelites more than he feared God. Saul saw what he did as partial obedience; God saw it as complete disobedience."

The mighty warrior arranged a private meeting with the king's son.

"What have I done wrong? Have I ever harmed you or my nation? Haven't I always had your father's back?

Jonathan told him, "I'm sorry David. He can't be reasoned with. If you wanna live you'll have to go into hiding. I know one day you will be king of Israel, and I will be there with you. I am your true friend for life. I'm for you. Make a covenant with me that we'll always take care of each other and our descendants."

After Lambo's escape, Saul accused the prince of double-crossing him. He tried to murder his own son, but was unsuccessful. The king became a ruthless assassin killing eighty-five priests of the village of Nob where David had fled. Mr. Slice and Dice then ordered everyone in Nob, man, woman, child and newborn living there as well as all the animals to be hacked to death.

God's chosen king heard about the sadistic slaughter and blamed himself for the massacre. "I shouldna put those priests and innocent victims in harms' way," he grieved. "I'm responsible for this horrible event."

One of David's loyal friends corrected him. "No, you're the one with God's heart for the people. A true leader cares more for the needs of those under him than his own desires. Saul doesn't care about anyone but himself."

The royal psychotic called all of Israel to go to war against Lambo. David was in the town of Keilah. He sought the Lord praying, "Lord, will Saul come here? Will the men of this town turn me over to the King?"

The Lord instructed him, "Saul will come with his army. The

men of Keilah will betray you to save themselves and turn you
over to the king."

Time and time again the shepherd sought the Lord in
prayer. The Great Shepherd kept leading, guiding, warning,
and protecting the hunted general and his army. The Covenant
Keeper actually allowed Saul and his men to fall asleep in a cave
where Lambo was staying. He crept up upon Saul. His men
quietly rejoiced.

"This day God has delivered this nut job into your hands."

David skillfully cut off part of Saul's robe but left him and his
military unharmed.

*Now the King will know for sure I'm not his enemy,* David thought.
*God has proven me innocent.*

He cried out to Saul. "Why do you listen to lies? Today God
delivered you into my hands and others encouraged me to kill
you, but I didn't. It was in my power to take revenge on you.
Look at the border of your robe. The Lord will judge between
us."

Saul trembled to realize how close he had come to dying.
"You've rewarded me good for the evil I would've done to you. I
won't seek to harm you anymore."

The demon-possessed leader kept his promise for awhile.
Once again the tormented king listened to the lies of the enemy.
"David wants your kingdom. Better hit him now or one day he'll
take you and your whole family out."

The double-minded ruler hunted God's anointed repeatedly. Each time the exiled captain chose not to retaliate, even
though Saul broke every promise made to David.

The nation of Israel was again besieged by the Philistines.
Their armor and weapons were greatly superior to the Jews.
Saul wanted to know God's plan for his nation but the prophet
Samuel had died. God did not answer Saul in the way or time
frame that he wanted him. Even though the murderous king

knew communication with the dead was prohibited by God, he chose to search for a witch to call up Samuel's spirit.

The medium of Endor did not know she was dealing with the king of Israel. She held a séance and a spirit came up out of the earth. Saul perceived that it was Samuel's spirit. The spirit lied and told the frightened ruler what all spirits that are contrary to the Holy Spirit will say. "God won't listen to you. He has departed from you forever. There is no hope. You have gone too far. There is no forgiveness or repentance for you." The fraudulent spirit masquerading as Samuel also told the paranoid leader. "Tomorrow you and your sons will be with me. . . "

That word also turned out to be a lie. It would be *three* days before the king and Jonathan died. Saul attempted suicide. He fell on his own sword and fatally wounded himself. An Amalakite finished the job. As a Jew, he knew God had forbidden witches, séances, and mediums in the laws given to Moses. The scriptures warned of the curses that would come upon anyone undertaking such practices.

The Bible tells us that Lucifer, who became Satan, was cast out of heaven. He took one-third of the angels with him. The fallen angels became known as demons or evil spirits.

It does make one wonder what would have, what could have happened if the Israeli ruler would have dared to believe God's words of mercy and forgiveness. Would the Lord have turned things around for someone even as sadistic as Saul?

*"Has the Lord as great delight in burnt offerings and sacrifices, as in obeying the voice of the Lord? Behold, to obey is better than sacrifice, and to heed than the fat of rams. For rebellion is as the sin of witchcraft, and stubbornness is as iniquity and idolatry. Because you have rejected the word of the Lord, He has also rejected you from being king"*
*-1Samuel 15: 22-23*

For more info on the Royal Mad Man and Lambo read the book of 1Samuel.

# CHAPTER 5

# Giving Hell a Heart Attack

*"Remember what we do in life echoes through eternity."*
                                              *-The Gladiator*

THE crazy king ordered him whacked, but he had won the hearts of the people. In fact, four hundred men of Israel joined the young warrior to give him protection and make him their next king. Most would have described them as losers. All of them were distressed, in debt, and discontented. Not a lot of strong military material to work with. But Lambo saw beyond their weaknesses. He knew the God-potential that was in each of them.

Saul's orders were, "Murder that little back-stabber at close range. Make sure he's dead; or you'll be killed, by me!

And what was the shepherd's crime? The royal crazy heard the ladies singing a silly tune.

"Saul has killed his thousands. David has killed his tens of thousands. . . " Who could imagine a simple song would start a war, but it did.

The first time the renegade king of Israel came after David, his army greatly outnumbered the shepherd's. Many of the men were in great fear and trepidation. It was their first battle. One of the company moaned, "I think I'm having a heart attack."

David thundered back at him and the rest of his troops. "You're not gonna have a heart attack; we're gonna give hell a heart attack!"

The young commander scrutinized his troops. Things looked pretty bad for the sorry bunch.

*These men are having a major meltdown. They look like they're going to God's funeral. I've gotta make this group talk, think, and act differently. Lord of Hosts help me. Together we've faced more daunting challenges than this. Heavenly Father, give me wisdom and a plan.*

David started working his men hard through military drills. He'd run them up and down the mountains. He taught them how to be skillful with swords. Prior to David, the Philistine nation had controlled Israel and taken away almost every sword and potential weapon that could be made of iron. The only one in all of Israel with swords was Saul, his sons, and his personal armor-bearer.

David was able to acquire swords and weapons of warfare through the relationship he developed with the new Philistine king.

Lambo instructed his men in hand-to-hand combat and wrestling skills. He developed their discipline. The shepherd turned general, also helped his men to "praise the Lord and pass the ammunition."

"We're fighting a spiritual battle, as well as a physical one. We're fighting the good fight of faith. Don't look at the fact that we're always outnumbered. See with your eyes of faith. If God is on our side, who can be against us?"

The brilliant, military strategist kept increasing the difficulty of the physical training. He drilled them until their insides were like coals of fire.

"It feels like I'm dying." One of the men protested, "What are you doing to us Lambo?"

"I'm saving your lives," the young garrison commander growled. "They far exceed us in number, so we have to far exceed them in skill."

As the troops observed their leader, they also learned to call upon the Lord and seek him for courage and direction. The complaining, cowardly group became fierce in conflicts. The young general's bravery and faith was contagious.

What was most perplexing to the men was David's refusal to whack a wicked leader. "He's God's anointed. I won't kill him or do him harm. I'll defend myself and my men, but I'm gonna leave his revenge and judgment to God."

The men marveled. *Constantly, this man's life is on the line, but he always fights fairly even when his enemy doesn't.*

The demons that controlled Saul were now speaking to him constantly. "Kill that rotten little punk. Take all your troops and squash him like a bug. He's dangerous to you. He wants your kingdom."

Saul gathered all his troops and surrounded David. The huge number of soldiers had him trapped. The hordes of hell rejoiced. "Now we'll get this troublemaker out of the way permanently. We'll take Israel out through their own crazy king."

The Lord of the Armies gave the young warrior a way of escape over and over again. The Prince of Darkness trembled at his faith and tenacity. All the legions of hell were having a heart attack! "How do we stop this miserable little Jew? We have no defense against his prayers and praise."

Lambo's troops increased. He was a captain that inspired the faint-hearted to become lions in the tribe of Judah. In spite of the greater numbers of men, they became experts in camouflage. They knew how to disappear into their surroundings when necessary. David's brilliant covert operations brought the army great victories.

When the garrison started to grumble, David would motivate them. "I've been an underdog most of my life. It's a good place to be. Being the underdog teaches you not to be overly confident. You must rely totally on God's strength and direction. The Lord has always seen me through to the other side of victory. We are more than conquerors. No fear allowed here!"

The heavenly, inspired melodies of triumph their leader played caused the men to go so far beyond what they thought they were capable of. The former group of whiners became winners. The earlier wimps became known as the mighty men of valor. Other nations feared and respected them.

Lambo stood in awe at what God had done in his life. The once scorned and despised shepherd boy had become a king. Impossible but true. With God the impossible became possible. The Lord even exceeded far beyond what David would have dared to dream. He recorded his victories and losses. The writings continue to inspire the hopeless and downtrodden to dare to believe that with God they can overcome anything.

> *Deliver me, O Lord, from evil men: Preserve me from violent men, who plan evil things in their hearts; they continually gather together for war. They sharpen their tongues like a serpent; the poison of asps is under their lips. Keep me, O Lord, from the hands of the wicked; Preserve me from violent men, who have purposed to make my steps stumble. The proud have hidden a snare for me, and cords; they have spread a net by the wayside; they have set traps for me. I said to the Lord: "You are my God; hear the voice of my supplications, O Lord. O God the Lord, the strength of my salvation. You have covered my head in the day of battle"*
>
> *(Psalm 140:1-7)*

CHAPTER 6

# The Minister of Israeli Affairs

*"She would tempt the devil himself."*

*-The Godfather*

H E had become a legend in his own time. Unfortunately, he had also become a legend in his own mind. This tough guy fought and won illustrious victories for his country. The men of war would do anything for him. The ladies swooned in his presence.

God appointed and anointed him king. It was springtime and once again his flourishing country was at war. Every foreign nation wanted what Israel had: the Ark of the Covenant, incredible favor, and success. Israel's blessings provoked other nations to jealousy. Even though it was the season for kings to go to war, David decided to stay at home in his palace.

*I know in my gut I should be going with my men. God I know you want me out there to help win these battles, but I'm going to stay home just a little bit longer. I'll go . . . eventually.*

One late afternoon as he was walking on the rooftop of his spacious dwelling, he spotted her. She was one gorgeous fox. This beautiful woman was also on her rooftop taking a bath.

*She's drop-dead gorgeous. Who is this naked lady?*

Lambo asked his servants about her. "What is her name? Does she belong to anyone?"

His staff told the leader, "Her name is Bathsheba. She is the wife of Uriah the Hittite. He is a mighty warrior for Israel."

*He's away. I just gotta have this babe. I'll just send for her and we'll have one incredible weekend together. I'm king. Whose gonna stop me?*

By this time David already had more than one wife and several girlfriends called concubines. He chose to ignore the inner voice of God trying to warn him. Lambo sent his servants to bring her to the palace. He had one phenomenal weekend with someone else's wife.

"Listen, I know you're a married woman so this can't continue. Let's just keep this our little secret, sweetheart. No one will ever know."

How shocked David was to find out two months later that Bathsheba was pregnant with his child. *Oh no, no one must know she's pregnant. All the men are at war. She'll be stoned and maybe me along with her. I'll send for her husband immediately. He'll go home, sleep with his wife and our little indiscretion will be taken care of.*

The Hittite was a man of great honor. He was a general in Israel's army and he knew while his men were out fighting for their lives, he couldn't be lying with his wife enjoying what every other guy was being denied. Uriah chose to sleep outside the palace with other servants.

The king was having the Hittite watched. Word was brought back to David how Uriah had denied himself out of respect for his troops. Lambo was getting frustrated. He ordered his staff to get the general smashed so he would go home to his wife. Even though he got drunk, Uriah had more integrity than the leader of his nation. He still wouldn't go near his wife.

Once again, word was brought to David that the Hittite would not go home. He hastily scribbled a note to another general to place Uriah on the front lines of the hottest battle and then withdraw from him and his garrison. An honorable man died that day along with a group of soldiers, betrayed by their own leader.

David was relieved to find out that the man who could expose his sin died. The king let Bathsheba have her time of mourning, and then quickly sent for her to become his wife.

David's latest wife bore him a son; he rejoiced to know he had another boy by his beautiful brand new wife. Everything in life was going great until the prophet Nathan came to the king with the word of the Lord.

"There are two men in this nation. One is rich beyond comprehension and the other is poor. The impoverished man had only one sheep, while the well-to-do man still has a count-less number of sheep. The poverty-stricken man loved and cherished his little lamb. He treated his sheep with tenderness and kindness. The affluent man took the one little lamb the poor man had. What do you think should be done to this rich man?"

David's anger exploded at the injustice. "Kill that rotten scum!"

The prophet pointed at the king and roared back, "You're the man. God caused you to win battle after battle. He anointed you as king. The Lord delivered you from the hand of Saul and all who came against you. He made you successful in everything you did. God planned to give you even more, but because you have despised the Lord and his covenant, you have opened your-self and your family up to wickedness of every kind. How could you forget how good the Great Shepherd has been to you?

"Did you think you could hide what you've done from God? You caused a faithful man and his troops to be killed. The Lord calls what you have done murder. You've caused great reproach and shame for your people."

Instant conviction hit the Minister of Israel. "I've sinned against the Lord."

Nathan responded, "Because of your true repentance, you
will not die. Your son is going to die and evil will come upon
your family."

Shortly after the prophet's visit, word came to David, "Your
baby is dying. If you want to see him while he is still alive, come
quickly."

The king fell face forward on the ground. A year after his
great transgressions, David prayed to the Lord he had once
known so well. He begged for the life of his child, and stayed
lying on the ground day and night and refusing all food. On the
seventh day he saw his servants whispering and he asked, "Is the
child dead?" With great fear and trepidation his staff replied,
"The child is dead."

The king of Israel arose, washed himself and went into the
house of the Lord to worship. He then requested food. Everyone
around him was astonished. "Why are you worshiping and eating
when you should be in mourning?"

The penitent leader replied, "I know how merciful the Great
Shepherd is. I fasted and prayed for my son, but he is gone. I
can't bring him back, but one day I'll go to him in heaven."

The Lord turned away his wrath from the fallen leader. The
king still lived with the consequences of his sin, but God had
compassion on David and Bathsheba. He gave them another
son they named Solomon. The child grew up to be the next king
of Israel and became world-renowned for his great wisdom and
insight that his parents imparted to him.

Following his great transgressions, God called David a man
after his own heart. The psalmist went on to show others the
way to true forgiveness. Wiseguys, good fellas and sinners of
every kind have found mercy and encouragement by the words
Lambo wrote in Psalm fifty-one after his horrible fall.

*Have mercy upon me, O God, according to your lovingkindness; Blot
out my transgressions. Wash me thoroughly from my iniquity, and*

*cleanse me from my sin. Then I will teach transgressors your ways, and sinners shall be converted to you. For you do not desire sacrifice, or else I would give it; The sacrifices of God are a broken spirit, a broken and a contrite heart-These, O God, you will not despise.*

*-Psalm 51:1-2, 13, 16-17*

# CHAPTER 7

# The Preacher Who Went to Hell

*I could go to hell for the lies I told for you!*

*-Italian Saying*

GOD'S directions to the prophet were very clear. "Go to Nineveh. The stench of their corruption has come up before me. Cry out against their violence and evil ways. Tell the people I am going to destroy their city and all who live in it."

The preacher, Jonah, raged against God and the assignment he had given him. "I don't want to go. I hate the Ninevites. Don't you remember what they did to the Jews? They're murderers without mercy. They tore open the bellies of our expectant women. They killed young and old, feeble-minded, disabled and Jews in the prime of their youth. I'm not doing it."

The prophet boarded a ship and sailed in the opposite direction of Nineveh to Tarshish. Jonah fumed when he thought about what was being required of him. *I've got to get away from the presence of God. I don't want to hear what He has to say. Jehovah is so unfair. Why should I have to preach to my enemies? Let someone else do it.*

The Lord sent a great tempest to toss the prophet's ship.

The wind and waves were so ferocious the ship was breaking apart. Each mariner prayed and offered sacrifices to every god they could think of. The storm grew worse, but Jonah was sound asleep in the bottom of the sea vessel. The captain awakened him, "Don't you know we're all about to die? What kind of fresh head do you have that you could sleep at a time like this? Get up and call upon your god. Maybe you can pray to a god we haven't thought of."

Jonah struggled to get to the top of the ship. The waves were beating violently against the vessel. Men were being slammed about. The mariners cried out, "Someone is responsible for this tempest. We gotta find out who has brought this curse on us. We'll cast lots to see who it is."

Lots were cast and it came down to Jonah. The ship men angrily accused him, "Who are ya? Where ya from? Whada ya done to cause us this trouble?"

The backslidden preacher confessed, "I'm a Hebrew. My God is the maker of heaven and earth and all that lives upon the earth. I am also a prophet fleeing from the presence of the Lord. This typhoon has happened because I raged against God and refused to do what he told me. As a result of my defiance, I've put everyone else's life in danger. Throw me overboard so that you can live."

The terrified sailors shook when they heard that Jonah's God was the God above all others. They didn't want to harm a prophet so they rowed against the tempestuous waters trying to get to land. Their situation intensified.

"I told you it's my fault you're in this mess. Cast me into the ocean and the storm will stop," Jonah shouted above the roaring storm.

With great anxiety, the crew flung the Hebrew into the sea. They cried out to the prophet's God, "Please don't punish us for this man's sins. You know we are innocent!"

Instantly a great calm came over the wind and waves. The

tempest was stilled and the sun shone brilliantly. Each man on the ship knelt and gave reverence and praise to the Lord.

Jonah fought to stay afloat, but the undertow was too strong. Currents swirled over him. Waves and breakers beat him relentlessly. He struggled like a wild animal to keep from drowning. The backslidden preacher was filled with horror as a monstrous sea creature opened it massive mouth and headed toward him. The huge fish swallowed him whole.

The acid from the beasts' belly was burning him from head to toe. He struggled for breath and finally became unconscious. Inside the fish, a gargantuan demon pulled the preacher down even further, descending with him into a greater darkness than he'd ever seen. The man who fled from the presence of God now realized he had gone to the regions of the damned.

As he continued to lower levels he saw an enormous inferno of flames. The rebellious preacher saw countless numbers of tortured souls burning alive. Satan and his cohorts filled the stenched air with evil laughter as the anguished shrieked in pain. Their tormented screams were the most horrible cries he had ever heard. It made Jonah feel like he was losing his mind, but his senses were more intensified than they had ever been. He also was on fire. His body seared with mind blowing agony.

The hopelessness, darkness, and anguish were more than he could bear. The burning prophet screamed in desperation from the depths of hell, "God forgive my willful, disobedience. I've been a fool. Give me a second chance and I'll go wherever you want me to go."

Hell quaked when God spoke. The hideous, evil being released Jonah from his claws. The prophet found himself back in the belly of the great fish, as God commanded the sea creature to spew out his repentant servant. Jonah was vomited out of the fish's body close to shore. Several people were on the beach to witness the shocking scene. The runaway Hebrew was covered in seaweed and vomit. His skin was burned and bleached from the internal acid of the beast.

He staggered onshore gasping for breath. The prophet, who had just been burning in hell, was now burning with the passion of God, the Father. He cried out to everyone he saw, "Turn or burn. Repent. The Lord has seen your wicked, ruthless ways. He hates the sins you delight in. God is going to judge this city in forty days. Hell is a real place of eternal torment and torture. I have seen it. That's where you're headed when you die. Soon all of you will be destroyed. Cry out to the one true living God for mercy."

Terror gripped all who witnessed the incredible incident. Surely this Jew, who was their enemy, had to be from God. News of the awesome event reached the palace. The king commanded the citizens to put on sackcloth, fast and repent for their sins. He published the prophecy of coming destruction and quickly sent out messengers to every part of his country.

The Ninevites responded with deep remorse and begged God for forgiveness. Jonah went from one end of the country to another carrying out his assignment from the Lord. After preaching to the entire country, the prophet sat on the beach awaiting the day of judgment for Nineveh. Jonah sat and sulked when he saw the nation of wicked inhabitants was not destroyed.

Ninevites became believers in Jehovah and completely turned from their sordid ways. The appointed day came and because of the true sorrow and repentance of the people, God chose to show mercy and grace to the people who were guilty of horrific acts.

Jonah sulked because his enemies were not destroyed. The Lord asked him, "Is it right for you to be angry because I didn't kill all these people?"

The prophet responded, "I have a right to be angry. I'm so angry I want to die!"

God answered him, "Shouldn't I care about the welfare of one hundred and twenty thousand people who don't know their right hand from their left? How quickly you forgot the mercy I showed you."

*I cried by reason of my affliction unto the Lord, and He heard me; out of the belly of Hell cried I, and thou heardest my voice.*

*Jonah 2:2*

# CHAPTER 8

# The Shakedown Artist Who Walked Away from It All

*Better the devil that you know, than the devil you don't know.*
*-Italian Proverb*

L EVI was the oldest son from a large Jewish family. He was also called Matthew by his family and friends. In harvest season, he labored in his father Jacob's vineyard before the sun came up until long past its' going down. As a little boy, he exerted much effort to ease his Papa's workload, but there was always more work to be done. Matthew pushed himself until his fingers bled and his young muscles ached. He knew he couldn't complain because his dad was doing all of the most back-breaking jobs.

Jacob's calloused hands and back were deformed because of the years of hard labor. Even when it wasn't grape harvest there was still so much work for the father and his son to do. The soil had to be fertilized and worked. The vine branches had to be cut and tended to. There was also a vegetable garden that required constant care.

In addition to all the other work, the family kept a small

amount of farm animals to feed their large family. Most of the siblings were too young to do any real work, so the bulk of it fell to Matthew and his dad.

He couldn't fathom why his dad worked so hard, but the Romans didn't seem to have to work at all. They just came into his father's grape vineyard and took however much they wanted without even asking. He noticed they didn't even have to break a sweat to do it.

"Papa, they just took the last of the eggs and . . ."

Jacob shot a harsh look at his son. He motioned for him to be quiet.

Matthew remained silent until the soldiers left.

"Why, Father, can they take whatever they want? They took one of our goats also. Mama needs milk for the family."

Jacob quietly said, "One day you'll understand my son. Until then, never ever question or argue with a Roman soldier."

The Romans were well-fed and clothed. They fueled the imagination of a young boy with their impressive armor and uniforms. Levi loved the authority with which they walked.

He enjoyed pretending to be one of them.

*What is it like to take whatever you want without paying for it? What exciting places have they seen? What faraway countries have they been to war with? What does it feel like to ride a horse? Have they experienced riding on a ship?*

As impressed as Levi was with the soldiers, the people that impressed him most were the tax collectors. They were the best dressed and the richest. The tax collectors were also referred to as the Black Hand, *La Mana Nera.* Pretty well-dressed women would be fanning the heads of the tax collectors. They would be handing them drinks or feeding them grapes.

Matthew thought, *they don't have to work. The only thing they do is collect money, lots of it. Beautiful women wait on them all day. What a job! This is what I'll do as soon as I'm old enough.*

Many times when Levi would go to marketplace with his

father, he would first have to stop at the tax collector's booth. His father would have to give the tax collectors a large amount of the family's hard earned wages. *Why?*

*La Mana Nera* didn't have to exert effort to get money. They just collected other people's cash all day long.

"Papa, why can't you get a job like that? You wouldn't have to work so hard and Mama would have nice things to wear."

"Levi, you must not ever be like the men from the Black Hand," Jacob said angrily. They're publicans. They're criminals. They steal from their own people. What they make is blood money."

Levi's curiosity got the better of him. "But Papa if they are criminals then why don't the Romans arrest them?"

Jacob wearily answered, "One day when you are older my son you will understand this also."

But as Levi grew, so did his admiration for the Black Hand men. He couldn't understand why his own people hated them so much. The tax collectors had it made! Matthew knew what he would do for a living when he became a man. He was going to be a shake-down artist for the tax collectors. He wasn't exactly sure what a shake-down artist did, but whatever it was he was going to do it.

Jacob was concerned about his oldest son's fascination with a group of men he despised. Levi knew his father disapproved of his high regard for the publicans, but he decided he wasn't going to spend the rest of his life like his father. He was going to live the rich life. He was going to be the one with servants. None of the tax collectors Matthew was acquainted with had deformed backs or blistered hands.

Levi's mom, Rebecca, had a beloved family friend and neighbor named Ruth. Ruth's husband, Bartholomew, had contracted leprosy. The man was exiled from the community. He could no longer provide a living for his wife and little ones. Rebecca and Jacob helped the young family as much as they could, but Jacob did not bring in enough money to support two households. Rebecca's friend Ruth was forced to move to a slum area where the family would be allowed to beg for food. The children could also see their father from afar.

Sometimes Ruth would come back to her old neighborhood to visit her beloved friend, Rebecca. She would pour out her frustration and bitterness as they visited.

"I hate the Romans. Worse still, I hate the tax collectors. Look at what they have done to us, their own people. My husband is a good man. He was always a hard worker, but the shake-down artists took almost everything he slaved for. They kept demanding more and more. Bartholomew finally paid their heavy extortion fees because they threatened to harm me and the children if he didn't. It left us with very little, and then we found out he had leprosy.

"It is so degrading for the children and I have to beg for our meals. I can only see Bartholomew from afar, but I can see how rapidly he is deteriorating. I know it breaks his heart that he cannot even provide for his own family. I often wonder if my husband had not paid these human leeches if the children and I would still have our home. I wish God would come and strike them all dead."

Rebecca was shocked by her friend's talk and bitterness. Ruth had always been the type of person that loved everyone. She was one of the most generous caring people Rebecca had ever known.

*Why had this happened to her and not the tax collector? Why did her friend have to suffer so when sinners were living such plush lives off the backs of good people? Still, how would I feel if it were my husband Jacob and the children and I were living in an unsafe neighborhood, begging on the streets?*

Another thing that greatly concerned Rebecca was her oldest son's interest in the men from the Black Hand.

Levi began to spend every free moment he could with the

men from *La Mana Nera.* Any time they needed something, Levi would volunteer to get it for them. He would even steal them some of his father's best wine. The Roman tax collectors were impressed with the young teen's stolen merchandise. They recognized how much his father Jacob detested them yet here was his son rushing to meet their every anticipated need.

Matthew had also seen the darker side of tax collecting. When someone couldn't or wouldn't pay he witnessed the brutal way they were treated by Roman organized crime. "Pay up or we'll break your legs. Better still we'll break yours and your mother's legs."

The tax collectors realized the young man had witnessed the whole scene.

"Sorry kid, he's loaded, but he just won't pay. If we don't make him pay, we get in trouble with Rome and then they come get us. *Cappish?*"

Matthew didn't like it, but it was still better than the way his father had to slave to make a living. And besides that, very few people could tell the Black Hand what to do. Mostly, he watched as they made their own rules.

The men of the Black Hand cunningly crafted a plan to see where the young man's true loyalties were. They asked him to rob more wine and livestock from his dad. They were well able to pay and they realized Levi's family could not afford the loss, but they wanted to test his loyalty. The eager to please young man passed every test. He always went above what he was asked. The men of the Black Hand were well pleased. They took note that he was someone they could make use of in the future.

One day his favorite tax collector was short-handed of body-guards and asked for Matthew's help at the collecting booth. He proudly stepped in. After years of carefully observing he knew just what to say, "Don't disrespect the publican. It's his job, okay? Pay him what you owe or else. . . . If ya point ya finger at me, I'll cut it off and shove it down your throat. Whada ya mean ya can't pay? Since when is two broken legs an excuse? I don' wanna hear it–I got problems of my own. Sell something or whatever, but get me the gold. Ya got one day to do it. If ya not back by sundown tomorrow, I'll wrap those crooked legs around ya throat."

Levi sensed the approval of the other shake-down artists. *Yes, I'm their man. I've passed all their tests with flying colors. I'm a "made man"!*

His family and neighbors were horrified. His father Jacob couldn't believe what his friends were telling him about his own son. The young man argued with his dad.

"Papa, I will not be a fool like you. I will be rich. I will have power and respect. You have chosen this way, but it is not the way I will choose. I will control my own destiny."

His father threatened to never speak to him again if he pursued this path of greed and destruction. His mother, Rebecca, begged her son, "Matthew these people are our neighbors and friends. Should you work with the enemy of our people to rob them? Do you know how dangerous this work is?"

Their firstborn coldly said, "I know how to take care of myself. Been doin' it since I was a kid. I'm very strong from all the years of working on the farm. This is my life. I'll do whatever I wanna do."

Levi moved out that day. He didn't care. His dream was not going to be stolen from him. His family stopped speaking to him that day. His mother's dear friend, Ruth, would not even acknowledge him as he she passed him to visit his mother. He became dead to his family and friends.

Levi did indeed become rich. He had the house and servants that he had always wanted. But he did not marry. He wanted someone like his mom Rebecca but the respectable Jewish girls would have nothing to do with him. He acutely missed his siblings and parents, but he had no intention of living out the rest of his life as a loser barely getting by. He loved the feeling of gold in his hands. Even though he had lots of it, it couldn't keep him warm or feeling loved at night.

Even though he didn't have a wife, he'd had many beautiful puttanas. He kept looking for the woman that would bring him fulfillment, but he didn't find her. The lines he used to get the girls were sounding more hallow each day.

"Hey doll-face, you're lookin gorgeous today. Here's some money to buy yourself a new outfit. I'll take ya out on the town."

All the loose ladies left him with a huge void in his very prosperous life. He hadn't expected this. Why, when he had everything he'd ever wanted, did he feel so bankrupt emotionally? He was wealthy. He didn't like forcing money out of people, good people, like his parents. He wasn't supposed to feel lousy. He had it made, why did he feel so guilty?

The charm of his new life quickly wore off. Emptiness kept growing inside of him, until he could barely stand the loneliness and lack of fulfillment.

One day his mother's friend, Ruth, actually stopped to talk to him. "Levi, have you heard my husband Bartholomew is back at work?"

The shake-down artist was astounded.

"But how is he working? I heard he lost several fingers due to his leprosy."

"He did lose his fingers, Matthew. A man named Jesus not only healed him of leprosy, but new skin and fingers grew out and now he is totally whole. I wanted you to hear our family's good news. You should go and see the Healer for yourself."

Levi carefully pondered his conversation with Ruth. He had heard strangers tell of miracles and he always wrote them off as nuts. But he knew Ruth and Bartholomew personally. He had seen Bartholomew's hands with the missing fingers. He had been so sick. Now he was healed and working. No one could fake this type of healing.

A few days later Matthew did go to hear Jesus speak. He saw the miracles and healings. He rejoiced with the people that were healed. All had a wonderful story to tell, and he listened intently to every one of them. Levi knew the Nazarene was the real deal. He felt his compassion and kindness. It had been a long time since Matthew had experienced kindness.

He was truly glad for the people but saddened by the life he was now living. He wished he could also be one of Jesus' followers but his sinful life told him otherwise. The truth was, he now hated being a shake-down artist. For days he thought about the Master and his followers. Matthew had the affluence but they had the peace. He longed for the life that could have been.

One day the Healer stopped at Matthew's tax booth. "Follow me, Levi. My Father has need of your service."

*My service?* Matthew could scarcely believe his ears. *Why would God want someone as rotten as me?*

Levi learned later, as he became a disciple of Jesus that people like him were exactly why Jesus came to the earth. A short time afterward, Matthew joined Jesus and the other disciples and he made a trip back to his parent's humble home. He timidly knocked on the door. He did not go empty handed.

"May I come in?" he asked his astonished parents.

"How are you my son? Ruth told us of her last meeting with you," Rebecca said.

"Mom and Dad I want you to know how sorry I am for all the reproach and disgrace I've caused you and our family. I've done so many things I'm ashamed of, but I am no longer a publican. I've become a follower of Jesus and I am one of the twelve. I have truly seen the Light and changed my ways. I know I can't pay for my mistakes but I did bring a bag of money with me to help with any extra family expenses."

His shocked mother and father looked at one another is disbelief.

*Was this their greedy son who would not even share any of his posses-sions with his younger siblings now offering to give the family money unsolicited? Was this the son that had despised their way of life, walking away from the job that made him rich?*

Yes, Jesus was truly a miracle worker. He had healed one of their best friends of an incurable disease and recreated his destroyed body parts. But he had also healed their son's greed and gave him a new life. The Healer of broken lives had restored their family as well. The parents' joy returned. They had spent years living in hell on earth, terrified about what might happen to their son. He was out of organized crime. They also experi-enced serenity for the first time in a very long time. The Master Physician truly did all things well.

> *And when the Pharisees saw it, they said unto his disciples, "Why eateth your Master with publicans and sinners?" But when Jesus heard that, he said unto them, "They that be whole need not a physi-cian, but they that are sick. But go ye and learn what that meaneth, I will have mercy, and not sacrifice: for I am not come to call the righ-teous, but sinners to repentance."*
>
> *Matthew 9: 10-13*

# CHAPTER 9

# The Traitor Mob Boss

*Some people you can't reason with 'em; you just gotta hurt 'em.*

*-Mob Saying*

E had a feeling in his gut. Something was going down today. *Something big.* Zacchaeus finished his breakfast, leaving olive pits and orange peels for the servants to clean up, and then walked over to the front door. Cracking it open, he blinked in the blinding morning sun as he spotted a cloud of dust in the distance, moving up the road toward the gates of Jericho.

Someone was coming; a person of importance. He could tell by the excited chatter of his neighbors, who had dropped what they were doing and were piling out into the streets.

*Who could it be?* Suddenly, his heart began to pound. *Can it be that man my insiders have been whispering about?*

Zacchaeus slammed the door behind him and ran out into the street. *JESUS.*

"Get outta my way, or I'll kill yous all!" he yelled, shoving his way through the gathering crowd.

The Mob Don, Zacchaeus, was not a welcome sight in the bustling town of Jericho. He had become super wealthy by racketeering, lying, and cheating his own people. He ruled by violence, intimidation, and threats. Respected and feared by other wiseguys, he made a fat living off the backs of the poor and oppressed of his day.

Zacchaeus ran a thriving, slick and excessively greedy establishment. His racketeering business was well organized and tightly structured. He was the chief tax collector. He was the head of everything financially for the Roman government. The Roman government didn't care how he got his use fees; as long as they got their tax money first. The Romans placed him in the position because of his strong-arm collection methods and his reputation as a ruthless collector. He not only collected taxes from the Jews, but he amassed a fortune from all the extra interest he forced out of his people. In addition to that income, he received a cut of the profits from every other tax collector because he was the Boss of Bosses.

The common people feared and despised him. Fellow mobsters looked up to him. They wanted to impress the Godfather.

Zacchaeus was small in stature, but he compensated for his size by operating in fear and control tactics. Machiavelli could have learned some tricks from him.

He climbed the ladder of corrupt success by being more aggressive and cold blooded than everyone else in the Mob. He had people beaten, robbed, and even put on ice when they couldn't pay his exorbitant, inflated interest rates. The Good Fellas called it juice money. Whatever they could add to what was owed, was theirs. Caesar's government okayed their collection methods.

On this morning, Zacchaeus had only one thought in mind as he elbowed his way through the crowds gathered on the street. *I gotta check out this guy, Jesus!* No one was cutting him any breaks, though, and there was no way this short guy was going to see over the heads of the townspeople.

An idea flashed into his brain, and he raced ahead of the crowd. His sandals slapped the pavement as he quickly headed for the tall, sycamore tree on the corner. Its low-hanging limbs stretched over the roadway where Jesus was heading.

Zacchaeus scrambled up the tree and settled into a crook in the branches for the perfect view.

How it stunned the crowd and religious leaders when Jesus stopped under the tree where the hated tax collector was hovering!

Zaccheus' heart was pounding in his ears as Jesus paused momentarily and then looked up into the tree. Their eyes met.

The crowd waited for this amazing prophet to call fire down from heaven and destroy the dreaded crime boss, the number-one enemy of the people. But He didn't do it. Instead, Jesus called up to him,

"Zacchaeus, come down! I'm coming to your house to eat with you today."

The people were stunned. Their jaws dropped in amazement. They murmured to one another,

"What is wrong with Jesus? Doesn't he know what type of man this is?"

Jesus knew exactly who he was dealing with. He knew even more about Zacchaeus than the crowd did! He was well aware of the corruption, usury, and violence. Jesus knew about the gambling and prostitution this crime boss was into. But he was also conscious of the potential of this organized crime boss.

Jesus wasn't interested in his sordid past. He wanted Zaccheus' future.

When Jesus extended mercy to the lowest of the low, he changed the man's destiny. Jesus saw him as he could be. Because of the great mercy shown to him, Zacchaeus became the man God always intended for him to be. He changed because he had a personal encounter with a loving, compassionate God. That encounter revolutionized a gangster's sorry life.

As the Godfather, he had absurd amounts of money, but his life was empty. He had the best house, servants, great food, lots of mobster friends, and easy women to keep him company, but he had no peace. He was always looking over his shoulder to see when his past would catch up with him. He didn't sleep at night. He stayed awake wondering if tonight was going to be the night when he would be taken out or beaten unmercifully. Fear and emptiness were his constant companions.

The Light of the World invaded his life and his meaning-less days were over. The heavy weight of his past was gone. The corruption and sick lifestyle were over. Zacchaeus had peace–real peace–for the first time in his life. He was free! He couldn't believe the love he had for the people he had used and abused for so long. Greed couldn't control him anymore. His Savior brought him a freedom and ecstasy he'd never dreamed of. He became a generous man with a purpose and a destiny.

"From now on Jesus, I'll give half of my goods to the poor. And for all those I cheated, I'll repay them four times the amount."

The Maker of heaven and earth sought out one little despised worm of a man and gave him back his self respect. Jesus performed many miracles that left people in awe, but some of the greatest miracles took place on the inside of men and women's hearts.

Their lives changed in an instant, because the Son of God had radically changed them. Forever.

*"For what shall it profit a man, if he shall gain the whole world, and lose his own soul?"*

*Mark 8:36*

Wanna know more about this Boss of Bosses? Check out Luke 19.

# CHAPTER 10

# The Kid Who Needed a Good Beating

*Tell me who your friends are and I will tell you who you are.*

*-Italian Proverb*

**W**HAT a drag! *This temple stuff is so lame. Thank God, it's the Sabbath. I won't have to work at the Old Man's business today.*

The rebellious young man rolled his eyes at the ceiling as the Rabbi continued to read from the ancient scrolls. Today the synagogue leader was reciting the Proverbs.

"Listen to me, my son! I know what I am saying; listen! Watch yourself, lest you be indiscreet and betray some vital information. For the lips of a prostitute are as sweet as honey, and smooth flattery is her stock in trade . . ."

The would-be heir couldn't believe what he was hearing.

*My Father just quoted this crap to me this morning. This very same thing. If this is you trying to speak to me God, I'm not listening, do you hear me? If you do exist, I'll make you a deal. You leave me alone and I'll leave you alone. Besides, I don't believe in you, so I don't have to do anything they tell me you require.*

The Rabbi continued to recite the proverbs.

"But afterwards only a bitter conscience is left to you, sharp as a double-edge sword. She leads you down to death and hell."

The spoiled brat bit his cheek to keep from giggling out loud.

*Yeah, sounds like lots of fun to me. Loose women, people who like to party!*

He wondered if the Teacher would ever shut up.

"For she does not know the path to life. She staggers down a crooked trail, and doesn't even realize where it leads. Young men, listen to me, and never forget what I'm about to say: Run from her! Don't go near her house, lest you fall to her temptation. And lose your honor, and give the remainder of your life to the cruel and merciless; lest strangers obtain your wealth, and you become a slave of foreigners."

The rich youth looked at his Father. His Old Man was hanging on every word the rabbi was speaking.

*How can he think this is interesting? He just lectured me with this passage. Or maybe my dad just gets off torturing me and my brother this way, although my sick-in-the-head older sibling may actually enjoy this. Perhaps he's just pretending, so he can get in real good with Papa.*

The wealthy widower, Solomon glanced at his rebellious youngest named Thomas. The teenager was yawning loudly.

*My son, where did I go wrong with you? I know things would be much different for you if your Mother, Tikvah, had lived to raise you. Maybe I should have remarried so that you could have had a woman's influence to guide you along the way. There was just no one to compare to my Tikvah . . .*

Thomas now turned his full attention to his older brother, Titus. He twisted his face away from his Old Man, crossed his eyes, and stuck out his tongue. Titus stifled his urge to laugh out loud. The comical scene went unnoticed by Solomon. There were many other temple members who were noticing though. They glared at both young men to let them know their disapproval.

The young heir knew how the villagers felt about him. In front of his dad they put on the big act. His father employed half the town in his marble and tile business. No one was stupid enough to tell Solomon to his face they couldn't stand his son.

The rich dad had seen to it both sons were well-trained in every aspect of his business. He had traveled with both of his children to Rome to show them how to select the perfect tiles and slabs of stone. The successful business owner taught them how to broker the best deals.

"Never appear too anxious while negotiating for prices and quality. Always invest part of the earnings with bankers. Stay aware of your profits and losses at all times."

Solomon displayed by example how to treat employees and servants. His kindness in the community was legendary. If one of the workers had a hardship of any kind, the wealthy owner saw to it that they had extra finances or time off. He was greatly loved by the people of Jerusalem.

It was on one of those trips that Thomas had developed a plan. He loved the city of Rome and the lasciviousness of the people living there.

*I'm gonna live just like these Romans. Father always tells me and Titus this is our business, learn it well. I have learned it well, and I will be more prosperous than my dad. I won't give to every servant that comes with a sob story. I'll cut down on expenses and have more to spend on me. Why shouldn't I ask for my half now, I've earned it.*

Thomas waited. It was harvest season. The business was flourishing and all were rejoicing at the prosperous year they'd had. Solomon was rewarding his workers with a celebration party. After the evening festivities, Solomon's youngest came to him.

"Father I've spent years working for you and learning every aspect of the business. It's time for me to go out and start my own enterprise. I'll set up closer to Rome to do my work. You said half this business is mine, so how about we settle up our financial affairs in the morning? I want to leave before winter sets in."

Solomon's face mournfully reflected his sadness.

"But son, this company is already prosperous with plenty of room for growth. If you'd like to move into your own home I understand, but stay with an already established business that works . . ."

Thomas knew the heartbreak he had just caused, but he didn't care.

"Papa haven't you always taught me to keep my word? Are you now going to go back on yours?"

"No son, I'll give you your half first thing in the morning."

Solomon's baby boy couldn't sleep all night thinking about the great life that awaited him.

*No more temple. No more rules. No more boring business. I'm rich and boy do I know how to spend it!*

As the sun was appearing, Thomas was already up and dressed in his best linen robe. His father noticed the candlelight coming from his son's room and knocked. His youngest stood so tall and regal looking.

*Wasn't it just yesterday,* Solomon thought, *he was a golden haired toddler asking a million questions? When did I go from being my son's hero to someone he despised?*

"Son this is your inheritance. Be careful Thomas, people are not always what they appear to be. If anything looks too good to be true, it's probably a scam. I will always love you and be here for you. Please send me word how things are going and where I can reach you."

Titus watched his brother and father. Part of him wanted to go with his youngest brother and have adventures but the other part of him knew he could never leave his father or his village. Jerusalem would always be his home.

The wealthy heir set out to have a good time. He wasn't going to start his own business immediately. They'd be plenty of time for that. First, he was going to enjoy life. Rome was a far way off but no one said he had to make it to the bustling city within the year.

*It's my time to be free. I'm gonna see all my dreams come true now.*

Thomas was treated by strangers with the same respect that his father had received. His costly garments, well-groomed appearance, and pricey jewelry were a walking advertisement.

He spent his first night on his own at a plush resort. There were beautiful, dancing women. Lots of them. All of them loose, exactly as he'd imagined. There were a great amount of well-to-do businessmen who knew how to have a good time, just like him. He continued on at the extravagant inn for quite some time. The beneficiary was very popular. He was invited to every social event.

The young heir discussed investing and business strategies with the other rich and famous people. After many girlfriends, he became captivated by one particular woman named Adah. In addition to being stunning, she was also sharp. Thomas shared his aspirations with her. "I know many of these men. Perhaps I can persuade a few of them to let you in on their ventures," she whispered and winked.

*I can't believe this fantastic fox wants to help me succeed.*

Through her connections, the naïve, Jewish son found many willing to help him invest his money. One of them pulled him aside to let him in on a secret deal.

"Thomas, I know of a ship owner who lost most of his fortune in a monsoon. He needs to rebuild his business quickly. He has established decades of successful trading routes with multinational enterprises. For a short term loan to acquire some new vessels, he will give you half of all the profits he brings in."

It was a lot of money he was asking for, but Thomas' greed caused him to jump at the chance to make lots of lucre without having to work for it.

"Consider it done," Solomon's son responded without hesitation.

After the young man turned over his cash, the investor disappeared never to be seen again. Adah consoled him. "Maybe our connection is still working out the details, don't worry sweetheart. You still have plenty of cash. Destiny brought us together. I would love you even if you didn't have a penny to your name. Your business savvy fascinates me. You are the most intelligent, brilliant man I've every met. Together, we'll jointly conquer the world."

The two of them although unmarried, became a couple. They traveled onward toward Rome.

Back in Jerusalem, Solomon yearned for his defiant son. If he heard any commotion outside his compound he would rush out with his heart racing to see if his Thomas had returned.

*No, it's not him. It's only the stone cutters.*

With each disappointment, the successful businessman became more despondent.

Titus hated the sorrow his brother had caused their father. As time went on, his bitterness toward his brother and his father grew.

*Why am I not enough for my father?* Titus thought. *If I had taken off like that ungrateful brat, brother of mine would he even miss me? Why hasn't he appreciated my faithfulness?*

The people of Jerusalem watched the father in amazement.

*What causes him to want that rotten kid back? How can he still love him? Why does he continue this daily ritual? When will he accept reality?*

They were now quick to give Thomas' dad advice. "If it was my son and he did return, I'd beat him within an inch of his life."

A fellow temple member told him, "You have grieved long enough. Have a funeral for him. We'll all come and mourn with you and he'll be as good as dead, then you can get on with your own life."

One of his long-time neighbors added more pain to his friend's agony, "Solomon, what you're doing this is not healthy. God gave you one good son. Face it, the other one's no good. He's a schmuck. Forget about him."

The grieving father fought to hold back a torrent of tears. *But he's not your son. He's mine. I will never forget him. Never could I stop loving him.*

Solomon couldn't forget the beautiful blue-eyed cherub he and Tikvah had welcomed into the world. He remembered his son's musical laughter that had filled their home with joy. His olive skin made his blonde curls seem angelic, almost heavenly. Friends and relatives told the proud parents, "We've never seen a toddler so well-spoken. He is so bright. This child will be something special one day."

Solomon recalled the day his precious wife died. This child who had just lost his mother told him, "Daddy, don't cry. I will always be your little boy. I'll love you forever. You don't have to sleep alone at night; I can sleep with you from now on."

The heartbroken husband heard Thomas telling his older brother, "Our mother has gone to heaven now. We have to be very brave and make Papa happy. We can't let him know how much we miss Mama. It will only make him sadder."

Tears of great loss ran down the cheeks of the downcast father's face. He loved both of his children, but things would never be right until both sons were with him again. He would never give up; as long as there was breath in him, he would pray for his prodigal son's return.

Thomas never did make it to Rome. One morning he woke up and Adah was gone. She had taken all of his money and possessions with her. This from the woman, who had promised, "Destiny brought us together. If you didn't have a penny I would still love you."

A severe famine hit the land. His fine jewelry was long gone. He was forced to sell the clothes off his back. In the middle of winter he was reduced to a loincloth and flimsy sandals. He was starving and freezing at the same time. He was now thankful to wear a torn up animal skin. He wore it on the frame that once displayed only designer clothing.

No work was available, so he begged a pig farmer to hire him for shelter. His job was to feed an unbeliever's swine, rotten food. His hunger was so intense even the putrid fodder looked good to him.

*My Papa's servants look wealthy compared to me. All of them are well-fed. My father would never allow one of his workers to be without warm clothing and shelter.*

*I always got so angry at him for his generosity, but I would be so indebted if someone would be that kind to me now. How far I have fallen.*

*I have been a prideful punk. I've lived like the pigs I am feeding. I wonder if my father could ever forgive me. I'll die if I stay here. He may turn me away but I've gotta try.*

Thomas started toward his home country that day. By the grace of God, and his Dad's prayers, he made it back into the arms of his loving Father.

*"And he arose, and came unto his father. But when he was yet a great way off, his father saw him, and had compassion, and ran, and fell on his neck, and kissed him. And the son said unto him, Father I have sinned against heaven, and in thy sight, and am no more worthy to be called thy son. But the father said to his servants, Bring forth the best robe, and put it on him; and put a ring on his hand, and shoes on his feet. For this my son was dead, and is alive again; he was lost, and is found."*

*Luke 15:20-22, 24*

CHAPTER 11

# The Gangster and
# the Phony Preacher

*"The saddest thing in the world is wasted talent."*

*- A Bronx Tale*

THE tax collector and the Pharisee were both in the temple at the same time. *Oh no, not again. Here I am a greatly admired man, and I have to be under the same roof with this scum. I'd love to have my muscle men throw him out for once and for all, but he gives so much cash to the synagogue. I'll just have to put up with him and his dirty money.*

The mobster stayed clear of the pious man up front. He had come to do business with God. He knew someone like him shouldn't be in this holy place. Yet, he felt a strange desire drawing him to this location. He didn't know if it was possible for someone like him to talk to God, but he had to try.

Years ago, he regularly attended the Sabbath services. As a tax collector, he was hated by the people, but he wanted to reach out to God. Simon hoped that one day he could work up the courage to talk to the synagogue leader about his circumstances. Maybe this man could give him some insight or council that could help. But, one Sabbath the Rabbi spoke directly about the Good Fellas.

As he addressed the temple members, his words were filled with contempt and total disgust for the Jews that betrayed their own people by becoming tax collectors.

"These gangsters must be despised by our community. We cannot associate with them. We are the righteous ones. They are the condemned. God wants us to hate them and their evil ways. Don't allow your children to associate with their children. They are sinful people. Anyone of them who thinks they can be saved has another thing coming. They will burn in hell for all eternity and their families with them."

Simon, the tax collector, got the message immediately. It was the last time he would ever attend a Sabbath service. He lost all hope that day that he could ever be saved. *Was it possible that if he gave generously to the temple, and he called on God when no one else was present in the holy place, that God would have mercy on his wife and children?*

The mobster thought back to what had brought him to this place. He never meant for it to be this way. He and his wife, Elisabeth, had a plan. They married young, but Simon had a good head on his shoulders and he had a strategy. He would use his strong body to help the merchants unload their ships. At night, and during slow times, he would study medicine. The doctor Luke took a liking to him. He told him he would help him become a physician.

But unexpected events kept his dreams from coming to pass. Simon's wife Esther gave birth quickly to one child after another. Their youngest became deathly ill. Luke told the anxious parents, "There might be a medicine that can help the baby. The problem is that the medicine would have to be imported and it would cost you more than a year's wages to buy it."

The young parents were beside themselves. They were both children of immigrants and neither set of grandparents had money. They had spent all that had to travel to this land. Money like that was impossible to get a hold of.

Simon wouldn't give up. There had to be a way. Many times when he was unloading cargo on the waterfront, crates would break open. Lots of the guys would steal the merchandise that spilled out. They would then sell it on the black market and make a rapid, big profit.

Simon joined them. It wasn't long before one of the waterfront bosses noticed Simon. He had a huge, muscular frame. His enormous shoulders could be very intimidating... and he was smart. *This guy had potential.*

The Head Boss of the docks approached him. "Simon I've been watching you. You're a sharp guy with great physical strength. I like the combination. Some of the other Good Fellas have also observed you. These merchants aren't paying us what we deserve. We have families to support. What do they care?

I've heard you have a sick child and a large family. I know you can use the tax-free cash. We'd like to make you an offer..."

Simon was swift to agree. *Yeah, I don't agree with their methods, but I can look the other way to help my family. Besides, I just need enough money to get my baby well and to help my family get ahead. Once I accomplish that, I'll get be out. I'll be back on track for my medical training. Then I won't have to deal with people like this.*

They made Simon an "Enforcer" on the docks. The easy cash was untraceable. He was able to get his baby well and to move his family out of the shack they were living in.

Simon's wife, Elisabeth, wasn't so happy with his new job. She didn't feel right about spending the money.

"Simon we had a plan. What has happened to it? You were going to use your brains, not your fists to make a living. I don't like those people on the waterfront. We have enough money now. Just leave these thieves. Let's start a new life."

Simon truly loved his wife and children. He knew the job he was in was dangerous, so he agreed to leave the waterfront.

Several hours later he returned home. Elisabeth was shocked by his appearance. He looked like he had seen a ghost. "What's wrong Simon, I thought you'd be celebrating? Instead you are acting like you've received news that a loved one has died. What is going on?

"I can't get out Elisabeth. I know too much. They said they'll kill me if I try to walk. I've reached the point of no return. There is no way out. I'll have to do this the rest of my life if I want to live."

Elisabeth could hardly believe what she was hearing. She wasn't allowed to ask questions about her husband's work. Even though she knew they were headed down a terrible path, there was no turning back. By stuffing down her emotions, life was bearable. She kept herself busy from sunup to sundown by focusing all her energy on her ever growing family.

Her husband rapidly advanced in the ranks of organized crime. It seemed like one day he was an "Enforcer" on the docks and the next he was a tax collector. Because of Simon's astuteness, he became a *Consigliere* to the Boss of Bosses, Zacchaeus.

Simon knew his boss was a ruthless man. The "juice money" he charged his own people was outrageous. But what options did he have?

Oh how Simon regretted his decision to become an "Enforcer". He never meant for this to happen. He gave very liberally to the temple, but other people's children were not allowed to play with his. The people he loved the most went through horrible ridicule and abuse because of his position. *Why hadn't he tried harder to find another way?*

Simon often studied the faces of his wife and children as they slept. *Would tonight be the last night he ever saw them?* He knew it was only a matter of time until one of his many enemies caught up with him. At least they would have enough cash to live a good life once he was gone.

Elisabeth and the kids had sat through the scorching sermon about tax collectors burning in hell. He already knew where he was going, but did the Rabbi have to say it in front of his children? The whole family was humiliated, so he stopped going to the Sabbath services with them. It was easier that way.

Simon never did stop going to the temple though. He went at times when he thought the place would be deserted. He bowed his head low and beat his breast. "God be merciful to me a sinner. I know I don't deserve it, but would you please watch out for my children. Have mercy on them God. They have nothing to do with the way I make a living. Please be merciful to us."

Unfortunately, he chose to go to the church at the same time as the religious leader. Simon could feel his hate.

The Pharisee saw the tax collector and showed his annoyance at once. *How was a man of his character and importance supposed to pray when such trash was in the back of the synagogue? Thank God he wasn't like this tax collector!*

The religious leader began his long-winded prayer. "Thank you God I'm not like this man. I don't break legs for a living. I'm not like the sinners. I don't steal. I pay my tithes. I fast twice a week. I observe the Sabbath. I deserve to be blessed. I'm a righteous man. I live a holy life."

The phony preacher and the tax collector were both unaware that someone else was also in the very back of the temple. The Son of Man had sat in the section of the synagogue unlit by candles. He did not want to be seen. He was there to observe.

His disciples sat quietly wondering why Jesus was so keenly interested in what was going on in front of him. He waited until both parties left before he also departed.

His disciples questioned him about his interest in the individuals they had just seen. Jesus told his disciples, "The religious leader prayed to himself. His prayers weren't heard by God because he wasn't interested in talking to God. He only prayed for others to hear.

The tax collector's prayers touched God's heart. God knew this man was truly sorry for the choices he made. The Lord will move through time and space to arrange circumstances to show mercy to a group of people that the religious leaders have written off as beyond hope."

"How will he do that Lord?" one of his disciples asked. Jesus answered, "He will arrange for Simon to be at Zacchaeus' house when I go there. Simon will receive the good news of the gospel. Salvation will come to his home. My Father will show him the way out even though he believes there is no way out. God will always provide a way for those who seek Him with all their hearts."

> *"And the tax collector, standing afar off, would not so much as raise his eyes to heaven, but beat his breast, saying 'God be merciful to me a sinner!' " I tell you, this man went down to his house justified rather than the other; for everyone who exalts himself will be humbled, and he who humbles himself will be exalted."*
>
> *Luke 18:13-14*

# CHAPTER 12

# The Man Who Got Caught with His Pants Down

*People who live in glass houses can't afford to throw stones.*

*-Italian proverb*

H E was one annoying little bump in the road, but still he had to be taken care of. One of their "wiseguys" did some investigating. A particularly wealthy merchant had stopped giving them "silence money".

Originally, he had eagerly agreed to pay them money when they confronted him about his well-paid mistress.

The enforcers approached him, "We know all about your red light lady. We have so graciously kept quiet about this 'situation.' There is some talk among our "Family" that you are not keeping the law. Some of our elders have even spoken of exposing you. Of course that would be the end of life as you know it. God only knows what your father-in-law, Josiah, would do to you if he found out."

The merchant Saul was horrified. His father-in-law always said he was the son he always wanted. He was constantly telling him how proud he was that he was taking on so much responsibility in the business. Josiah had boasted to people that one day his son-in-law Saul would be in charge of the whole operation. He could not risk losing it all.

"I'll do whatever it takes," begged Saul. "I'll never see her again, I swear. I was wrong. Please give me one more chance to show I can change."

One of the crime family's "shake-down artists" spoke up. "We don't want to ruin you, Saul. We understand that you're a healthy, strong man with greater needs than most. Perhaps if you are willing to increase your giving to the temple, we could persuade the elders that it was just a misunderstanding. Of course you'd have to give the extra money directly to our enforcers so that the heads of the "Family" wouldn't find out"

Saul hastily agreed to pay the "hush money". He had paid them faithfully every single month. After six months, they increased the cash he had to pay. Several more months went by, and they were now demanding much larger takes. Saul was a greedy man, but he had been willing to pay to cover his indiscretions. Now they were demanding exorbitant fees. He didn't know what to do.

He went to Mary's that night. She always made him feel better. "What's the matter honey, you're so tense?"

He spilled out the whole blackmailing scheme to Mary. "Why should you have to pay? Don't you know how many of the syndicate are our customers? In fact, the chief priest is here every week looking for a new girl."

The merchant was outraged! "I have been paying all this bribe money and the Pharisees and Sadducees crime families are doing the same thing? How dare they! I'm not gonna give them another dime. And if they threaten me again with my father-in-law, I'll expose them."

Saul went through with his plan and stopped paying. The crime family now had to figure out how to get him to keep giving the pay-off money yet keep him from exposing any of them.

One of their mastermind scribes came up with the perfect solution to their problem. "After we make our move against him, we'll eventually get him to give us Josiah's business. We'll own that business one piece at a time. But for now, let's just mention the cash after we nab him."

The best part about this plan was that they could nab Jesus in the process. The "Family" could keep getting even bigger bribes from the merchant and bring the Nazarene down by means of the Roman government. What a genius this henchman was. He was worth every penny they paid him.

They approached his red-light lady, Mary. As planned, they would make her an accomplice without her even knowing it.

"We've been watching you. You have a unique gift to use discretion with your clients. For that reason, we have selected you for this special occasion. We want to recompense the merchant, Saul. He has done so much for our people. It's our small way of acknowledging his many contributions and accomplishments. We know you've been such an exclusive lady in his life. He has visited many other girls, but you're the one he always chooses. We will pay you ten times the normal rate for this event. We ask only one thing of you: do not tell him because we want our treat to be a surprise. If you help us, we'll send a lot more clients your way."

Mary was shocked. *These men don't care about what I'm doing. They just wanted some bribe money along the way. After all, everyone has their own racket. Saul has it all wrong. He needs to stop being cheap and pay these men what they are worth to him. They aren't out to get him. He got himself all upset, and here they are trying to honor him. Surely they'll work with him concerning the pay off money. It would be great for Saul to be honored at the temple in such a significant way. Plus it would be great for me to get so many high class clients.*

Mary was so flattered that these wealthy men of importance had even noticed her. They were not condemning her but asking for her help. Very few people had ever offered to help her. These well-respected men had spoken so kindly to her. She was not used to kindness.

Saul's mistress had a very tough upbringing. Her earliest recollections were of the men her mother brought home. She had never known her father. Her memories of the many men that came to her home were that of abuse. Her mom rented her out to them like a piece of furniture.

"You can do anything you want to her as long as you give me the cash before you begin."

Mary remembered the pain of rape and abuse. She remembered the smells of drunken men on top of her. She remembered screaming to her mother to help her as pain seared through her little-girl body, but her mother had already left their dwelling. She was left alone, helpless to defend herself against the animal that had paid to do these atrocious things to her.

For the first time in her life, Mary felt approved of. These noteworthy men needed her. She quickly agreed to remain silent and help them. She would send word the next time the merchant was coming to see her.

Saul came within a few days of their meeting. She let him know how excited she was to see him. Mary told him she just needed to get a message to one of the other girls she worked with. Her friend swiftly brought word to the crime families. She thought she was helping Mary. Little did she know…

The door burst open. There stood all the high ranking members of the Temple Cosa Nostra. Mary hadn't expected this. Neither she nor Saul had any clothes on. She tried to hold the blanket over her body. They ripped the covers off of her. The bodyguards restrained her as all of them stood staring at her naked, shivering frame. Saul was allowed to dress.

"Saul you have played us for fools. Haven't we kept quiet about your puttana? And how do you repay us, by forgetting our generosity? Now we're going to have to expose you to your father-in-law, wife, children, and the entire temple. They will have to decide what to do with you."

Saul was beside himself. "No, please I'll pay. Whatever you ask, I'll make it up to you. I'll give you the cash right now. I just came back from a trip. Josiah has no idea what I've received. I'll give you the bribe money up to half of what I just made".

"All or nothing. You're going to disappear for awhile. Tell your father-in-law an unexpected emergency has come up and you have to leave immediately".

Mary breathed a sigh of relief as disgraced as she was at least Saul was paying their demands. How shocked she was when they started dragging her naked body outside. She managed to grab the small linen curtain off the window.

She screamed, "Saul help me. You've just paid their demands, tell them to let me go. Please, they are hurting me. Where are they taking me? "

Saul just stared at the ground. He remained silent. He rationalized his decision like any coward would. *I just bought my ticket out of trouble. I can't open myself up to additional problems. I'm a beloved, highly recognized member of the community. My wife and kids can't know about this. What if my father-in-law found out? Mary knew the risks she was taking when she got into this business. She is a grown woman. Let her take care of herself. I can't endanger all that I've worked for. "*

They pulled her by one of her arms and sometimes by the legs. Sometimes they yanked her by her long hair. Mary struggled to keep the curtain over herself. Saul ignored her cries the same way her mother did. The one man that she thought cared about her was just like all the others.

They dragged her before Jesus. There were thousands present, and she was only partially covered.

Her entire body shook. Why hadn't Saul helped her? He told her he loved her. Her mother had never told her that. She believed him, but like each person she had ever looked to, he abandoned her.

Saul stood cowering at the back of the crowd. Both crime families were demanding judgment from Jesus.

"She was caught in the very act of adultery. The law says we have to stone her. What do you say, Teacher?"

Jesus didn't answer them.

"Look at her. She doesn't have any clothes on. Do you approve of adultery?"

Jesus stooped down and wrote on the ground with his fingers. Everyone in the crowd wanted to know what he was writing. The Teacher wrote the names of all the girls they had on the side. He wrote the sins they had committed that very week.

Finally Jesus picked up a large rock. "Let he who is without sin, cast the first stone."

The Temple mobsters looked at the ground. They looked at all their sins written in the sand. *How did he know? Would this Prophet expose them before anyone if they dared to cast the first stone?*

One by one, they left. Once again they had failed to trip up this amazing man. The crowd wondered why they hadn't stoned her.

Jesus reached for a large shawl from one of his followers. He covered Mary with it. Mary felt his kindness and compassion.

"Has no man found fault with thee? She answered him, "No man, Sir." Jesus spoke to her with such tenderness, "Nor do I, go and sin no more, Mary."

Mary could hardly believe what she had just experienced. The one the crowds called "Prophet" had just forgiven and defended her. She discerned that he somehow was well aware of the life she had lived. He showed her mercy instead of judgment.

Mary became a follower of Jesus that day. The large group that Jesus was traveling with showed her great kindness. They tended to her physical and spiritual wounds. The worst day of her life, turned out to be the best one she'd ever lived. Mary found her peace with a loving, gracious God. She truly was accepted and not judged by these believers in Jesus.

In the daily companionship of other believers Mary found the family and love she had sought after her whole life. She went on to live an incredibly fulfilling life, surrounded by people who truly loved her.

Mary set off to the red-light district one more time. This time she didn't go to make some quick cash. She went to tell the other girls there was a way out of the hell they were living in. A whole group of these unfortunate women went to see the Healer for themselves. Many of them went on to start brand new lives.

Saul left that day depressed and full of rage. He also felt doomed. He knew he was in debt to the Good Fellas and he'd never get out. The company that he had worked so hard for eventually became the property of the local mobsters. But he lost so much more than money and property that day. He lost his own soul. His whore became free and he became a slave.

*"Do not envy wicked men, do not desire their company; for their hearts plot violence, and their lips talk about making trouble."*

*Proverbs 24:1-2*

# CHAPTER 13

# The Judge on the Take

*If you want to get something done, be like the turd that won't flush.*
*-Italian saying*

THE corrupt judge sat on the bench greedily wondering how much he'd make today. He was pulling in outrageous amounts of money. It was a beautiful setup. Organized crime couldn't muscle in on his scam, and the Roman government didn't know about it. It was a sweet financial deal.

The judge looked at the schedule and tried to figure how much he could squeeze out of the criminals that were appearing before him that day. Even if they were falsely accused people, he'd be glad to look the other way and convict them if the one fingering the accused, came with enough cash.

As the shady official looked at the docket, he gleefully realized today was a day with a lot of potential for cool quick cash. He had a couple of guys accused of murder, robbery, tax evasion, soliciting a prostitute, and then he saw her...

*Ya gotta be kidding me. Not again. Not this one. This broad never gives up! She's driving me freakin crazy. She comes week after week with the same relentless demands.*

The woman's questions were blatant and embarrassing.

"Avenge me of my adversary. You know this man cheated me out of my rightful inheritance. You promised me you'd take care of it and you didn't. I want what's due me. I can't and won't pay you bribe money. Make this man pay. How am I supposed to live without receiving what my husband worked so hard to give me and my children? They're not old enough to work, and I can't work because of my injury. Give me and my children what this man swindled us out of. Did my adversary pay you to throw this case? Do you want all these people to know how shady are you?"

His assistant looked at him as if to ask, *do you want the court police to get rid of her?*

Everyone in the court heard her. She was bad for business. If the Roman government found out he was making all this money under the table without paying taxes, they could throw him in the slammer. He had blown her off time after time. Now people were starting to ask questions. Too many people could start sticking their noses in his business.

All the people in her village knew about this case. They could hear her praying intently while they were trying to sleep. At night, the loud praying of the widow crying out to God resounded in their ears.

"Avenge me of my adversary. God, you said you are my defense. You said you are the husband to the widow and father to the fatherless. You said you would be my advocate. Show yourself strong on my behalf. Deal with this crooked judge. Give him no rest until he does what is right."

*I can have some of my men work her over, but then again, what if it comes back on me? She's come so frequently that everyone is well-acquainted with this case. She's not given me a dime of bribe money. She knows how the system works but she refuses to pay. This stubborn, persistent widow is back to hound me again... And she's yelling louder than ever,*

"I want the justice due me and my children. Avenge me of my adversary. I'm not leaving until you do."

The lawyers were watching the corrupt judge to see how he would rule. *I don't fear God and I don't fear any man. But I do need this people to fear me. If I throw her case out, I won't make anything. Still, it will be worth it just to get rid of this nagging so and so.*

"I've made a decision in your favor, Elizabeth. The defendant has until sundown today to pay what he owes you and your children, plus interest. New evidence has come to light that proves he defrauded you. Let it be noted to everyone present and to Caesar that I am a just judge. I help the widow and the fatherless. The court will now adjourn for a half hour recess"

His muscle men were incredulous. *How could he rule in her favor when she never even offered to give him anything? This irritating woman had badgered and slandered him and yet he gave her what she wanted.*

The judge met with his officials and enforcers in his chambers. "I know what you are all thinking, but I had to do it. She was a nuisance. She was also very bad for revenue. I knew she'd never stop coming so I decided to get rid of her by giving her what she wanted. I can't stand the harassment anymore. Even though she aggravated the hell out of all of us, it was money well spent to get rid of her. Even though I hate her, I admire her determination."

The stunned court officials looked at him in disbelief. *Today was one for the books. This relentless little widow never gave up. She didn't care how many times the judge ignored her. She did what no rich, crooked official had ever done. She got the judge to avenge her without one penny of "pay off" money. She cried out to God and even a callous, fraudulent judge couldn't take the pressure that God put on him.*

*The hand of the diligent shall bear rule.*

*Proverbs 12:24*

Would you like to know more about the broad that wore the judge out? Read Luke 18:2.

# CHAPTER 14

# Opposing Organized Crime Families

*There is no honor amongst thieves.*

*-Italian proverb*

A DJUSTING the thick folds of his fine robe, the tall, aristo-cratic-looking man scanned the crowd of vendors spread out over the majestic temple steps. Chattering pigeons in cages, the smell of farm animals, and the metallic clink of coins mingled with the voices of buyers and sellers.

A faint smile crossed the man's face as he stroked his beard. *Business is good today. A little marketplace entrepreneurship is good for the economy. Better yet, it's good for me and mine.*

Strolling among the stalls, he caught the glance of another observer, also impeccably dressed, standing in the shadows. He stifled a scowl and nodded a stiff greeting. Annoyed at having to share his territory, he was resigned to the reality. But he didn't have to like it.

Pharisees and Sadducees. Everyone in Israel knew how much these two groups hated each other. What everyone did not know is that both groups were organized crime families. Their front or legitimate business was religion. Being a member of one of these corrupt families was like receiving a license to steal.

Both crime families were extremely well organized and ran their enterprises like military operations. Their secrecy and *omerta*, code of silence, kept the ordinary people in the dark concerning the truth on many levels. If some poor slob was brave enough to question the way they ran their business, he might wind up with a good beating or worse still some "cement shoes".

Sometimes a trouble-maker would have a little "accident," arranged by one of the crime families. The families got their message across loud and clear.

"Mind your own business. If you see something you shouldna seen, you just say you saw nothing and nobody gets hurt, *cappish?*"

It wasn't just beatings and unfortunate accidents that these wiseguys set up. Neither family was above "icing" someone to protect their "interests".

The wealthier of these two families were the Sadducees because they had a greater influence with the temple and they considered themselves to be the high class aristocrats. The Sadducees crime family believed that only the first five books of the Bible counted. Of course, if you could make them count $ differently, they'd frequently overlook the majority of offenses. Their favorite mobster expression, "Forgetta 'bout it."

The temple was where both of these groups made the bulk of their money. The second family was the Pharisee crime family. They had more run-ins with the law than the Sadducees family because they were constantly trying to rewrite the laws. They represented themselves as *the* Law, and in almost all cases they were *the* Law. Unless a person was totally "stunad," stupid, or crazy, he did not dispute what either family said, even if they had said something totally different just the week before.

The good fellas were treated like gods. Another of their favorite wise guy expressions was, "God helps those who help themselves!"

And help themselves, they did indeed. They had made so much money under the table, it enabled them to buy designer clothes for themselves and their families. They lived in palatial estates with magnificent furnishings and breath taking gardens. Their food was top quality and, of course, they had countless servants waiting on their every whim and desire.

Even though these opposing families despised each other, they still had a healthy respect for one another. The families cautiously agreed,

"You steer clear of our business and we'll steer clear of yours. You run your racket as you see fit and we'll take care of ours."

Both operations faced the typical problems mob fronts face, but with all troubles considered, their operations were running smoothly and profitably until a certain Nazarene came along. He was not afraid of either group, nor would he give them the respect and honor everyone else did.

He challenged both families publicly and denounced their ruthless racketeering. For the first time, the Sadducees and Pharisees crime families were in agreement. The punk, a Nazarene named Jesus, had to be dealt with by means of a unified mobster takedown.

But how were they gonna take him down?

*The wicked watcheth the righteous, and seeketh to slay him. The Lord will not leave him in his hand, nor condemn him when he is judged.*
*Psalm 37:32-33*

# CHAPTER 15

# **The Trouble-Maker**

*"Keep your friends close, but your enemies closer."*

*-The Godfather*

He was a simple man with nothing special about his appearance. And he wasn't afraid of anyone, not even the crime families. Nor would he give the wiseguys the attention and praise they craved.

*This Nazarene, Jesus, must have his own scam going on,* they thought. They just couldn't figure out how he was doing it. He mesmerized huge crowds, healed people, performed miraculous feats with nature, and raised the dead. The trouble-maker didn't charge to get into his meetings, and this Jesus character refused payments for any miracles he performed. He wasn't flattered by their attempts to get on his good side. The one the people called Master, refused all types of bribery. Worse still, this renegade Nazarene seemed to really know the law.

In spite of the fact there was no love lost between these crime families, they decided to arrange a meeting. The Nazarene, Jesus, had cut into both families' huge takings. People were no longer coming to them and paying enormous amounts of money for their phony prayers.

"You know that wealthy widow, Sylvia, who comes so loyally each week? She's been coming to me for years with prayer petitions for herself, her parents, her kids, and every other jerk request. She has stopped coming. Sylvia said the Nazarene told her to go to God as her Father and pray in Jesus' name. Who does this uneducated bum think he is?"

"I know," replied another wiseguy. "This Jesus is making me crazy! He actually thinks he is on the same level with God. That is blasphemy!"

The religious crime family members loved the honor and reverence all the people gave them. Oh, how they enjoyed the adulation of the crowds! They pretended to be holy and pious before the multitudes, and were outraged that Jesus dared to oppose them publicly. He refused to give the good fellas their due respect for the high positions they held.

Another thing Jesus did that really ticked them off was that he associated with Zacchaeus, another crime boss who was an enemy of all Jews and both crime families as well. Even though this enemy was also a Jew, Zacchaeus was a total sell-out to a non-Jewish related form of organized crime. He was a hated Jew because he was a traitor to his own people. He ran his own "shake-down syndicate" with the cooperation of the Roman government and neither crime family was given even a cut of the profits.

The Nazarene openly associated with prostitutes, crooks, and other low life scum. The enforcers tried to intimidate and threaten him. But the man had no fear! These powerful "crime families" were able to stay in existence because of the terror they instilled in the people. Now, this Nazarene was ruining their perfectly good enterprises. The families consulted with their legal experts: the scribes and lawyers. They were also known as the *Consiglieres*.

Their experts rendered their legal opinion. "Our best bet is to entrap Jesus into breaking the law–Roman law that is. We've already had him shadowed for three and a half years, and we still didn't find him breaking any major laws. Misdemeanors are not what we need. Misdemeanors will only send him to the joint for a few years and when he comes out he may be more popular then ever. Look at that other nut, John the Baptist. They stuck him in the joint and the people still believe he is a prophet. In some ways, the Baptist is more dangerous to us now."

The Pharisee and Sadducee families finally came to a mutual agreement. They needed some big time felonies to get rid of Jesus legally—and "permanently." Under the Roman government, a Jew could not sentence another Jew to death. That privilege was reserved for Romans only. The crime families needed some type of crime with meat in it.

They had sent the most gorgeous playgirls and babes of Israel to seduce him. All of their best "girls" wound up becoming followers of this Jesus. It wasn't like any of the wiseguys didn't have *comares*, mistresses on the side; they just wanted to expose this Nazarene publicly for doing the same things they were doing privately.

Jesus didn't take the bait.

They sent their mob soldiers to rough him up: instill some healthy fear in Jesus and then arrest him. But all of them came back converted!

"You gotta hear him! The man is amazing. He is making blind people see, and deaf people are totally healed. I've never seen anything like it in my life. This guy is amazing! I don't believe Jesus has a racket going on. I believe he's the real deal. You should go down and see him."

Some of their own high ranking members decided to go to one of his meetings. They would find out his tricks and watch for people that he had planted in the crowds. They would find out how he was faking these phony healings. The inner circle would expose him as a fraud.

They conspired together. "You watch the outer boundaries of the crowds. I'll watch him up close. You get your captains scanning the people to find the ones that claim to be miraculously healed. This Nazarene is going down!"

But with all their best efforts, they could find no flaws in his miraculous healings. In fact, some of them were finding themselves drawn into the Nazarene's circle by a powerful, wonderful presence. They felt his love and compassion for the people. His goodness transcended their evil. They somehow knew that he was aware of all their shortcomings and yet he loved them. Never before had they experienced anything like this.

They went back to report on all that they had seen at the Nazarene's meeting. Although all of them were at the same meeting, they disagreed with what they had experienced.

"He's a good man. I've never felt such joy in my life."

"Nonsense, he's a crackpot. He talks about God like he is personally acquainted with him."

"Maybe he is."

"Do you mean to tell me you believe in him, as well? The Savior will come from Bethlehem. He's a Nazarene. He's a sinner. Check out his 'old man'. See what this punk's father did for a living. See if you can find any scandals in the family."

"No one could do the miracles he does and be wicked. He has to be from God. We can't oppose what God is doing!"

That day a few of them even broke rank and joined his organization!

They had another emergency meeting. Their rival, Jesus, had to be stopped! The captains came up with a plan. They would organize a gangland execution and make it look like the ordinary Jews killed him for breaking their laws. They would incite a riot and have the common people throw him off a cliff. They came up with just the perfect place to make it happen. But the Nazarene somehow slipped away without being touched!

Once again they consulted with the *consiglieres* for legal council. Their best legal minds came up with a scheme to lure him into breaking Roman law. They would get him to say something against Caesar. So they sent their best men to do the job.

Turns out this Jesus was a genius! "Give me a coin, Jesus

commanded. "Whose inscription is on this coin?" The wiseguys replied, "Caesar's". "Give to Caesar what is Caesar's and give to God what is God's." He confounded their most brilliant "talent" and tripped them up instead. How did he always do it?

Another "sit-down" between crime families was arranged. They had their lawyers and scribes search the law to find a legal loophole to convict Jesus or at least discredit him so badly that no one would follow him. One of the preeminent lawyers spoke up,

"I've got it. I've found two statutes in the law to make the people stone him!" The first one he is in violation of is found in Deuteronomy 18:10-12. It states,

"There shall not be found among you anyone who makes his son or daughter pass through the fire, or one who practices witchcraft, or a soothsayer, or one who interprets omens, or a sorcerer, or one who conjures spells, or a medium, or a spiritist, or one who calls up the dead. For all these things are an abomination to the Lord . . ."

The lawyer continued with wicked pleasure, "Leviticus 20:6 states, 'And the soul that turneth after such as have familiar spirits, and go after wizards, to go a whoring after them, I will even set my face against that soul, and will cut him off from among his people'. "

Everyone from both crime families agreed that this would be their trump card. They would be able to turn the people against Jesus because he was a sorcerer, guilty of practicing witchcraft and magic, all offenses worthy of death. Of course they could not kill him themselves, but they had the evidence they needed to turn the common Jews against him. They just needed to get their best *goombas* on the job.

Huge crowds followed Jesus. They would stir the people up and get him stoned. He couldn't escape thousands of people against him. They would tell the people that God commanded his death because he broke so many of their laws.

But once again, their scheme did not work. The common Jews said he had to be from God because of all the miracles he did. He even fed the thousands that came to hear him on several occasions. Jesus was driving them out of business.

The last straw was the day he visited their temple and took a whip to the underlings working there. He overturned the money changers' tables and threw the scales and balances they had so carefully fixed to cheat the people. He chased away the vendors with their animals and wares and proclaimed, "Is it not written, my house shall be called of all nations the house of prayer? But you have made it a den of thieves!" (Mark 11:17).

"How dare he call our temple his house?" they raged. "And he called us thieves in public!" In order for the crime families' racket to keep working, the people had to believe they were holy and had some special power with God.

"This Nazarene has gone too far! Imagine the nerve of him. He's just an ordinary Jew, a carpenter, telling us what to do. He has to be stopped, but how?" Just when it looked like the good fellas were going to be driven out of business it happened. . .

*"Your leaders are rebels, companions of thieves; all of them take bribes and won't defend the widows and orphans. Therefore the Lord, the Mighty one of Israel, says: I will pour out my anger on you, my enemies!"*

*Isaiah 1:23-24*

# CHAPTER 16

# Dead Man Walking

*The devil always calls you what he is.*

*-Italian proverb*

THE Pharisee crime family was beside themselves with demonic delight. They gave their slanderous scoop to the *Israeli Enquirer*. The publication ran it as their lead story. The headline read, **Best Friend of Jesus Dead, Healer Refused to Come to Deathbed.**

People came out in droves for the funeral. Everyone had their opinion. A lawyer bellowed, "I always knew Jesus was a phony; now this proves it!"

A local rabbi complained, "Why didn't the rabbi prevent this; he healed all those people, why not one of his chief supporters?"

The religious syndicate made sure their men were fueling the gossip mill. Smearing others and defamation of character was their specialty. "Make sure we have a lot of wiseguys at the funeral. We'll say we're going out of respect for Lazarus. Mary and Martha will give us a big, fat donation for sure. They'll acknowledge us over that hypocrite healer, besides it'll be another great opportunity to spread more smut about the son of Satan."

The mobsters all turned out for the burial laden with jewels, gold, and their most somber mourning garments. What a show they made of their deep remorse and regret over the young man who had died. They hissed in the ears of the grief-stricken sisters and all who would listen, "What kind of heartless animal is this Jesus? When his friend needed him the most, he refused to come. Even today on the day of his burial he isn't here. He's a bloodsucking bum."

They instructed the good fellas after the funeral, "Stay in Bethany close to these two broads for their week of bereavement. Don't leave them alone. Let's see if this coward shows up."

Afterwards one of the followers of Jesus came and whispered something to Martha and Mary. Martha rose immediately. She collapsed in the arms of Jesus crying, "Lord if you have been here my brother would not have died, but even now it's not too late. I believe that if you ask God he will give us our brother back."

The Lord of Life replied, "Your brother shall come back to life."

The bereaved sister answered, "Yes, I know in the future he'll rise again with everyone else on Resurrection Day."

Jesus strongly responded, "I am the resurrection and the life, whoever believes in me will live again because I give them eternal life. Do you believe this Martha?"

"Yes, I believe that you are the Messiah, the Son of God, the one we have so long awaited."

She quickly left the Lord to call her sister secretly to come see their friend, Jesus. She knew the religious syndicate wanted to get their hands on him and, even though she didn't understand, she didn't want to endanger the Master.

Mary arose abruptly and left her home. The Black Hand members present followed her. "We have to put on a good display. She must be going to the tomb to mourn. Make sure you cry loudly and shed a lot of tears. The crowd needs to know how much we care."

*It was Jesus she was going to see.* "She is so hurt and angry with him. Let's watch this rich witch tell him off. This scandal will be great business for the family. Make sure you get several eyewitness accounts for the press."

Mary fell at the feet of Jesus. She wept uncontrollably, "Lord, if you had been here my brother would not have died. Why did you ignore our pleas for help?"

The Healer groaned and was deeply troubled. "Where have you laid him?"

They took Jesus to the tomb. The syndicate feigned concern for the sisters and wailed obnoxiously. Jesus wept.

Some of the Jews present said, "Do you see how much he loved him?"

The religious organized crime family members quickly turned off their tears and jeered, "Jesus loved him; He loved him so much he didn't even show up for his funeral! He claims to heal people all the time. Why didn't he heal his pal?"

The Healer's face displayed his agony over their unbelief and the corruption of the religious leaders.

He summoned strength from his Father and fearlessly commanded, "Roll the stone away from the tomb."

With horror Martha realized, *Jesus is beside himself, I'll have to take control of the situation.* "Oh Lord, we mustn't. He's been dead for four days, by this time he stinks."

The Master replied, "But didn't I tell you that if you believed you would see the glory of God?"

The *La Mana Nera* was only too happy to oblige Him. They had their muscle men roll the stone away. *Today we'll expose this phony prophet. He's gonna look like a complete fool.*

The enforcers were choking at the stench of the dead body. Although they had rubbed out many people, they never had to dig up one of the bodies after this many days. *What is this whack job preacher thinking? What does this Healer think he's gonna do with a stiff?*

Lazarus awoke free of pain. He was in Paradise basking in

healing warmth and love. The young man looked at his body. *I'm free of disease, whole, and complete. What's that fragrance? It's the most magnificent scent! And what is that sound? Never have I heard such flawless melodies. Even the laughter here is musical.*

*I've never been here before yet I feel at home. I'm cherished and accepted. This is the place Jesus was talking about.*

He felt two sets of arms slip around him. Tears of joy spelled down his face. "Momma and Papa, we're together again!" Glorious reunions of loved ones that had passed away took place over his time in Paradise.

His parents escorted their son to places of exquisite beauty. The follower of Jesus splashed in the Crystal Sea and swam with sea creatures he'd never seen on the earth. Majestic heavenly mountains greeted him. Flowers and lush landscapes were alive with color and life. Everything seemed to have a voice testifying to the greatness and goodness of God.

He was at perfect rest when an angel came to him and said, "You must go back, Jesus is calling you. Go and tell others what you've seen. Reassure them to not fear death or grieve for loved ones who have died."

Lazarus felt himself going downward toward earth. He heard the strong, clear voice of his friend Jesus calling, "Lazarus, come forth."

He felt himself slipping back into his body. Resurrection life and light burst forth into the dead body. Every organ, tissue, and cell was instantly recreated. Even though his body was bound, he was able to sit up and then stand.

The wind of the Spirit swept over the tomb and crowd. The air that reeked minutes before with the stench of death was now infused with the magnificent scent of the rose of Sharon fragrance. Lazarus brought the aroma of heaven back with him to the earth. Life triumphed over sickness, scandal and death.

Lazarus hobbled forth as Jesus commanded, "Loose him from those grave clothes and let him go free."

The friend of Jesus wasn't the only one to go free that day. Many syndicate members were also released. They believed. Even though all saw the miracle some religious leaders chose to not accept the Truth. Many didn't like God's messenger or his message. The religious leaders didn't want to change their way of thinking or their lives. Forgiveness and eternal life was being offered to all, but they wouldn't heed the voice of the Lord. The Black Hand ordered a hit on the dead man walking, but God protected him just as he had his Son.

Lazarus and his sisters went on to share what incredible things God had done for them. Their test truly became a testimony.

> *"I am the Resurrection and the Life: He that believes in me, though he were dead, yet shall he live."*
>
> *John 11:25*

For more info about the dead man walking, see John 11 and 12.

# CHAPTER 17

# The Set-Up

*"You are still pulling the strings."*

-*The Godfather*

S OME of the Sanhedrin syndicate secretly met. It was a "sit-down" by invitation only with the high priest, Caiaphas. After being introduced with a very grandiose overture, the head of the religious mob opened the meeting.

He had on his high priest outfit. The godfather of the Sanhedrin looked very pompous in his Egyptian linen garments. The rare gems sewn into his clothing made him look extravagantly ostentatious. He had to look the part. Caiaphas had to look like "the one" God Himself had given the ultimate authority to. He could not show any signs of weakness. Any that had their doubts about the decisions he was making, needed to know that if they argued with him they were arguing with God.

"Thank you all for coming to this unforeseen meeting. After much prayer about this matter, you were hand-selected by God to do this important task. I want to warn you once again that this is a private meeting that must remain *omerta*. Not everyone has the special insight and revelations about the law that you do."

He keenly observed the men assembled before him. He knew he had to choose his words with wicked, well-chosen wisdom. "Jesus has severely affected our profits. Many men who once gave generously to the temple are not giving at all now. Rumor has it that they are giving to that despicable Nazarene."

He portrayed the facade of a leader who truly cared about the state of Israel. Caiaphas wanted to represent the strength and honor of his high position.

*Just keep flattering them. Make them feel superior to everyone else and they'll do anything for you.*

He continued, "What makes our situation worse still is that this traitor has endangered our very way of life with the Roman government. We all know they barely tolerate our religious practices. It is my belief that Jesus intends to appoint himself king of Israel."

Some of the Sanhedrin was leaning forward, intently listening. Others were nodding their heads in agreement. Still others with fists clenched were scowling at the thought of what the trouble-maker was doing.

Caiaphas' chest puffed up with pride, he could feel their approval. The chief priest congratulated himself.

*You've done it! No wonder I was put in this position. I'm a master manipulator. I've won every one of them over!*

Caiaphas knew they were with him. He had them exactly where he wanted them.

"Herod is the only king that Caesar will allow. If this Jesus leads a rebellion against Rome, we will all be held accountable. As the high-ranking members of the Sanhedrin, we will be the most severely punished. They'll sell our wives and children into slavery. We'll be forced to give up our observance of the sacred laws. Our way of life will be forever lost. Our state will cease to exist. We can't allow this. If this man, Jesus, has to die so that our nation can live, so be it."

In spite of Caiaphas' arrogance and lies, his last statement was actually one that came from God. This man, Jesus, was willing to die for the nation of Israel. But unlike the religious syndicate, Jesus was not counting worth in dollars and cents. He was counting the worth of Israel in souls. Jesus was a stand-up guy. He knew the horror that was coming, and yet he faced his worst enemies without fear. They were among the very ones he was willing to die for...

They had the sworn affidavits from the syndicate's group of liars and cheats. The *La Mana Nera* finally had their ace in the hole. Their most damning evidence would come from one of his punk disciples, Judas. He would be their chief witness. He was drilled on what to say. The stool pigeon would arrange a time when the crowd was not around. They needed to bring Jesus in without causing a riot. *Let the games begin.*

> *"The wicked watched the righteous and seeks to slay him. The Lord will not leave him in his hand, nor condemn him when he is judged."*
>
> *Psalm 37:32-33*

CHAPTER 18

# The Rat

*"Your murderers come with smiles; they come as your friends."*
-The Godfather

ONE of his *goombas* came to them. This guy was willing to turn stool pigeon and traitor if they gave him enough money. Both crime families were in agreement. "Let's pay the snitch, Judas, the money. He'll be our top informant. We'll also find and pay witnesses to slander the troublemaker. One will lie and the other will swear to it. Beautiful."

With one of Jesus' very own turning state's evidence against him, they'd be able to take this punk out without any of them even getting their hands dirty.

"We can't risk getting defiled. It's blood money. If we dirty our hands, we can't be in the temple making all that cash!"

The families congratulated each other. "We finally got a plan without a hitch. This arrangement will help everybody keep his piece of the action. We'll pay our witnesses top dollar. We'll finally find out how this blood sucker, Jesus makes his wealth and does his magic tricks. His friend, Judas is gonna sing like a canary at his trial."

*Things were finally coming together. How great it was gonna be to get back to normal.*

Not everyone was happy with the plan. Nicodemus didn't mince words. "I was like all of you; I didn't believe this Jesus was

authentic. But I went to investigate and found him to be a man
of integrity. The miracles and healings were valid. I won't allow
this man to be lied about and slandered. We all make a good
living. We don't need to do this."

The high priest, Caiaphas, stepped in. "Of course we're
not going to lie about the Nazarene, Nicodemus. You misun-
derstood our intentions. Our scribes are speaking out of turn
because they have been so overworked lately. We simply want to
question Jesus when everyone is present. Naturally, we have our
concerns about what you call miracles and what we call magic.
Isn't this what our religious high court is all about? We seek only
justice and to know the truth. You do want justice and truth
to prevail don't you, Nicodemus?" Nicodemus left disgusted by
what he saw and heard.

Caiaphas motioned for his personal body guards. "Keep
Nicodemus and Joseph of Arimathea out of this. From now on
it's *omerta* when these two are present. When we see them we do
a *face contente*, we say yes, yes to their faces and when they walk
away, we do whatever we want."

Judas carefully watched for an opportunity to hand over
Jesus. The rat of the two-legged variety was the treasurer over
donations people made to support the ministry of Jesus and his
disciples. He tried to make Jesus see the potential for profit, but
he just wouldn't listen.

Judas rationalized his plan. *The religious rulers have their own
syndicate. They are making more money than God. Why can't Jesus
muscle in on their profits? People are willing to pay huge amounts of
cash to perform miracles. Word on the street is that King Herod will pay
handsomely to see Jesus do some miracles.*

Jesus refused all payment for healings and miracles. A group
of wealthy Greeks had traveled a great distance to see Jesus.

*Why didn't he hit them up for money? And what about the filthy
rich synagogue leader whose daughter Jesus raised from the dead? The
rabbi was beside himself with gratitude. There wasn't any amount he*

*wouldna paid for his daughter's miracle. Then there was that Roman centurion who had come for his servant. That guy was loaded! He'd have given anything Jesus asked him for.*

There were times that Jesus would accept money, food, shelter, and clothing for the group that traveled with him, but Jesus would never accept compensation for the signs and wonders he administered.

Judas had to admit, *I've never gone without since I met Jesus, but he gives every bit of the glory to God. He is too freakin' humble.* The more Judas thought about all the lost lucre, the more enraged he became.

*The Master is makin' me crazy, especially when he says, "Freely you have received, freely give. I only do the works my Father has sent me to do."*

Every time he said that, Judas got *ogeda*. His stomach was in knots over the amount of missed financial opportunities.

*Why is it okay for Lazarus, Nicodemus, and female followers of Jesus to be wealthy, but not me? That's his number one fault. A guy like Jesus will never get it. That's why I need to step in. If Jesus isn't interested in living the good life, that's his problem. Why does Jesus have to live so holy anyway? Can't he see that I have the skill to run our own racket? I'm not gonna let him stop me from makin' some serious chunks of change!*

Jesus was well aware of Judas' inner rage and struggles. He knew the God given gift Judas had for finances. Jesus wasn't against his treasurer having money. He was against money having him. He had prayed for his disciple, Judas to overcome his sin of greed many times. But even the prayers of Jesus could not supersede the will of his friend who was willing to sell his own soul to the devil to become rich.

The informant waited for the right opportunity, and it came shortly after he'd approached the Sanhedrin. It was Passover night. It was just the twelve and Jesus. The Son of Man spoke, "This night one of you will betray me."

Each one asked in astonishment, "Is it me Lord?"

"It is the one that I dip my hand in the cup with." As Jesus spoke those words, he and Judas were dipping there hands in the cup of wine at the very same time…

The traitor was shocked. *Jesus knew.* He even said, "Friend what you are about to do, do it quickly."

*Maybe Jesus understands that this is inevitable. He has to start working with the religious syndicate. I know he's the Son of God. I know he's innocent. But once the trial is over, Jesus will finally see things my way. The Master will see how much cash can be made. I'm really doing him a favor. Think of all the money we can give to the poor…*

The Rat, being treasurer, would see that he got his cut first. If he needed to use the poor as his racket, oh well . . .

What Judas didn't know was that the Sanhedrin planned to put Jesus to death. They played the little stool pigeon like a fiddle, and he never even suspected what they were about to do.

Something else Judas didn't know was that Jesus loved him so much, he was going to die for all the sins Judas had committed against him. He died so that his friend wouldn't have to go to hell. Jesus had explained the plan of salvation, but the rat never took it to heart. He didn't want to give up control of his life, not even to God. His way was too difficult.

Judas reasoned to himself, *Jesus is wrong. There's gotta be a better, easier way.*

It was only a few hours before, that Jesus had been washing the feet of Judas. Perfect love was still reaching out to him, hoping against hope that Judas would turn and repent, but he didn't.

Now the traitor greedily rushed to collect the money he would make for betraying the best friend he'd ever had.

The rat found Jesus in the garden of Gethsemane, just as planned. He had instructed the enforcers,

"Watch for my signal. I'll greet the Master with a kiss".

He approached the Son of Man. Their eyes locked. Judas

looked into the loving, heartbroken eyes of Jesus. He embraced and kissed him. Then, like all rats do, he ran as fast as he could to avoid what was coming.

The legacy Judas "The Rat" left to the world was the kiss of betrayal. Two thousand years have come and gone since then, but throughout the world it is still called "The Judas Kiss".

Good fellas use the Judas kiss to embrace an enemy they once called friend. The embrace is understood as a pronounced death sentence on the one being kissed. The name Judas will be forever associated with greed and the ultimate betrayal of a friend.

By the way, the money Judas so zealously sought did not bring him the good life he thought he would have. Within hours after "The Rat" received the money, he hanged himself.

*"Faithful are the wounds of a friend: but the kisses of an enemy are deceitful."*

*Proverbs 27:6*

To read more about "The Rat," check out Matthew 26 -27 and Luke 22:48.

CHAPTER 19

# The Politically-Correct Politician

*"Politics and crime–they're the same thing."*

*-The Godfather*

WITH a vengeance he had fought and clawed his way up to the top of the Roman government. He mingled the blood of Jews with animal sacrifices and offered them to his gods to gain more power. This official took out vendettas on those who opposed him. Pontius Pilate bribed a lot of people on the way to one of the highest political positions of the Roman Empire. He viciously ordered the hits on many rivals, but that was the price he paid for success and just look where it got him! Being politically correct had never been his concern before he got to this post, but now that he had arrived, no Jew or competition was going to take it from him. He was willing to do whatever it took to keep it that way.

The servant shifted nervously as he brought his boss the news. The governor was a cruel, large, intimidating man. He was resplendent in military armor. His robe of Roman authority was full of medals and cords, symbolic of countless battles ruthlessly fought and won. Sometimes as entertainment, he punished Jews and servants just because he was sadistic and enjoyed hearing the screams of his victims as he had them tortured. He and his *goombas* would place bets on how long it would take for some poor slob to die after being tortured.

*Is he in another bad mood? How do I tell him the religious organized crime leaders are outside, demanding a meeting with him? Am I gonna catch a beating for these despicable, impossible to please people?*

"What is it Antony? I'm a busy man and your loud, obnoxious breathing is driving me nuts. Spit it out, quickly so I can get back to work."

"Sire, the Jewish elders and leaders are insisting they need to speak with you right away."

"Insisting? Who the hell do they think they are? No one but Caesar tells me what to do! What's their freakin' problem now? I hate these Jews! I want them in and out. Go get 'em and tell them I'm a busy man, way too busy for their bull ****."

*I've never worried about doing the politically-correct thing before I got to this post. Now I've got all the Empire looking over my shoulder. I gotta make sure I got my own butt covered. I'm forever getting ogeda worrying about the biased implications and popularity polls. A good beating and threats are much easier strategies to make people obey. With every evil eye on me, I gotta be smooth and slick. Who knows which soldier is a rat for Rome, just waiting in the shadows like a black widow spider, looking to strike at me when I least expect it.*

The *La Mana Nera* came in decadently dressed in their fine linens. Behind them stood a prisoner, bound with chains. The Sadducees and Pharisees feigned phony bows pretending to pay tribute to Pilate. Their grand gestures of honor and facial expressions made the governor smirk. *They're faces are as red as my wine. They must want something really big to be pouring it on this thick. Do they actually think for one second that I believe this mock bull ****?*

"What's going on? You think I got nothing better to do than listen to your ranting. I got my own headaches, I don't need yours. I got all of Judea to run."

One of the chief priests spoke, "Your most honorable sir, this man has broken the law, incited riots, and claims he is the King of the Jews. He deserves death and you know we cannot put a man to death under Roman law."

"What's he done? Why should I bother myself with your petty religious crime disputes?" Pilate scrutinized the prisoner. He didn't look fearful, nor did he look hardened or defiant. *They've already given him a beating, yet he looks calm, almost peaceful. And why isn't he defending himself?*

The thoughts of Pilate were interrupted by a hand-written message from his wife, Veronica. "Have nothing to do with the judgment of this man, Jesus. I had a horrible dream about him last night. I know he is innocent of all the charges these wicked men are bringing against him. I don't want you to be cursed."

The governor shuddered inwardly. He was an extremely superstitious man. *Veronica and her dreams. So often she is right on the money. I'm not gonna be cursed for these freakin' zealots. I'm gonna torture him for awhile. I just won't let my men kill him. After he's been made to feel searing pain, he'll talk–they always do. Rome can't condemn me on this one, he'll still be alive, at least while he's in my hands.*

After an intense whipping, Jesus was brought back to Pilate. The governor addressed the *Cosa Nostra* leaders. "Well, you got what you wanted, now get outta my sight."

Once again, the air was filled with shrill accusations. One of the *consigliere*'s pointed out, "He told us to cheat Rome out of its rightful taxes. He's guilty of tax evasion."

A scribe spoke up, "This rebel says he heals people, but he doesn't heal anyone. We know he uses magic tricks. He claims to work miracles over nature and death, but he isn't deceiving us. The people are stupid and ignorant. He accomplishes these things by sorcery, not by God."

Jesus remained silent. The Roman leader spoke up. "This is a matter of your law, not mine."

Finally, another of the chief priests said, "He claims he is the Son of God."

The governor almost gasped. "The son of god, which god?"

*Keep it under control, Pontius. Can't let them know how scared or superstitious you are. It would make you look weak in the sight of all.*

The brutal Roman punisher had a brainstorm. "Where's he from?"

"Galilee."

*Thank the gods, it's Herod's jurisdiction. Let him take the heat from Rome.* Pilate sent him over to the king, but Herod sent Jesus back accompanied by soldiers with a note. "Just like you, I beat him to try to get him to talk but he wouldn't. I think this guy's got Thursday missing. I couldn't find anything punishable by death."

Another moment of evil genius hit Pilate. *The Black Hand is jealous of this man's popularity. It's the Jews' Passover. I'll use their high holy day against them.*

"At Passover, Caesar releases one prisoner to the people to show the leniency of our government. Let your people decide."

*I'll bring him out to the crowd and they'll want him to go free and none of my enemies can stick me with anything.*

The governor brought Jesus and another prisoner named Barabbas out to the multitude. Pilate shouted to the crowds, "Who do you want me to release?"

They shouted, "Barabbas, Barabbas, Barabbas!"

Judea's ruler tried to reason with Jesus. "Don't you realize I have the power to set you free or have you killed?"

The Nazarene replied, "You could have no power over me except that God gave it to you. Therefore the one who delivered me has the greater sin."

Pilate shook at his answer and went out to the throng once again. "This man has done nothing worthy of death. I find him not guilty."

The governor did not know that the crowd had been bribed with big amounts of cash before Jesus was brought out to them.

The Roman leader asked the people, "What do you want me to do with your king?"

"Crucify him. If you let him go you are no friend of Caesar's. Whoever makes himself a king is no friend of Caesar's."

Pontius Pilate knew he had to keep his popular opinion poll numbers up in Rome so he chose to go against what he knew was the right thing to do. He delivered Jesus to the masses to be crucified. The ever politically-correct politician tried to cleanse his hands that day from something water would never wash away. He would never know another day of peace or happiness again. That was the ultimate price he paid for his political success.

*"To Jesus the Mediator of the new covenant and to the blood of sprinkling that speaks better things than that of Abel."*

*Hebrews 12:24*

# CHAPTER 20

# The King with a Thing for His Stepdaughter

*"He is defying you. His every act is an act of defiance. The mob sees this, and so does the Senate. Every day he lives, they grow bolder. Kill him."*

-The Gladiator

H E was a drunk and a glutton. Every female on his large staff qualified for a sexual harassment lawsuit. If the palace workers didn't laugh long enough at his jokes or they laughed too hard they would be severely punished or "taken out"–as in dead.

The psycho leader would ask, "Are they laughing at me? Everyone knows a king can't tolerate such belligerence!"

If they didn't foresee what he was going to want, God help them! The servant, who had the misfortune of being present when the royal ruler of Galilee was stung by a bee or bitten by a spider, was made to suffer for it. The Tetrarch invented the super-size meal long before the fast food industry.

An overflowing portion of food would be set before him. Herod Antipas' voice would boom, "Why you bringing me such little portions? Am I on rations? Don't you know a man in my position needs more food for energy? How do you expect me to function on these meager amounts? And how come this food doesn't taste good? You trying to kill me? You pathetic scourge of the earth, now I'm gonna kill you!"

Needless to say, there was a vast amount of unwilling employee turn over. He was always requiring new doctors as well. As the physicians kept disappearing, the new replacements smartened up. They told him exactly what he wanted to hear.

"Yes, your highness you need to keep drinking hard liquor in large quantities; it's good for you. Of course you need to eat excessive amounts of food and dessert; you have to keep up your vigor."

Herod questioned them. "Do you think the small amount of food and alcohol I consume is the reason I am not sleeping at night and have difficulty with my breathing?

"Absolutely, King you are the healthiest man in Israel."

The ruler of Galilee breathed a belabored sigh of relief. "Finally I've found physicians who know what they're talking about. These men are almost as intelligent as I am."

Herod was seriously delusional. The rest of the world saw a huge, hefty man with horrible manners and an insatiable appetite for everything he saw. When he looked in his reflecting glass he saw himself as an exact replica of the buff King David statue that stood in front of the palace.

*I'm a chick magnet. Every woman I meet wants a piece of me.*

Antipas wanted everything he set his beady little eyes on. He could have any woman in the kingdom he ruled–they weren't given the luxury of choice–but developed a fixation with his brother's wife, Herodias. One day he made a royal decree and took her as his wife based on the new law he just passed.

*I'm the king I can do anything I want and nobody better get in my way.*

Herodias didn't mind changing husbands even though she was still married. She liked being the new queen. Ice water ran through her veins. She was a shrewd, conniving woman. She used sex to get what she fancied. Herod's wife also hated John the Baptist and all of his followers. John had warned Herod, "It's not right to live with your brother's wife. She is not yours to have. Fear God and repent. Send her back to her lawful husband."

The queen added unforgivenss and bitterness to her already black soul. She wanted the prophet killed, but she knew she couldn't disclose her true intentions to her new husband. He liked and feared John. They often had long talks together while his wife secretly fumed.

*I despise this prophet. I want him destroyed. I've got to figure out a way.*

Herodias was cunning. The queen knew she'd have to be careful and calculating to get the Baptist killed.

As her daughter grew and developed as a young woman, Herodias saw the shameless, leering way Herod stared at her. *That's it. My husband now wants my daughter. So what, I'll still be queen. I'm tired of his grubby, disgusting hands on me anyway. Let him have her. I'll set it up. That Baptist will never condemn me again.*

"It's the king's birthday. Make sure my husband has plenty of booze. He works so hard to keep this kingdom going. I have a special surprise for him."

When she saw that he was plastered, she instructed her daughter to perform an incredibly seductive dance to sexually entice the king.

The royal ruler's eyes were glued to his stepdaughter. She had very little clothing on and what she did wear was see-through. The princess danced slowly and erotically, very close to the king. Almost foaming at the mouth, he gasped in her ear, "I gotta have you. I'm going nuts thinking about you."

He wanted to impress all the men present. Drunkenly he yelled, "Wasn't her performance amazing? Isn't she the most talented dancer you ever seen? What do you want my pretty princess? I'll give you anything up to the half of my kingdom."

The seducing stepdaughter quickly consulted with the

queen. She also had taken up her mother's offense. "Tell him you want the head of John the Baptist on a silver platter."

Brazenly she strutted back to the king, "Give me the head of John the Baptist."

A shocked Herod said, "But don't you understand? I'll give you anything!"

"I want the head of that false prophet." She then pouted and with great disappointment said, "My Tetrarch isn't going to go back on his promise is he?"

An embarrassed, regretful Herod sighed, "Give her what she wants."

After John was beheaded, angels of darkness began to harass the king. Accusing voices kept him up at night. His mood swings increased. One minute he'd be laughing with high-pitched hysteria and the next he'd be kicking and punching a servant for no reason.

Some of his staff became believers in Jesus. They cautiously tried to help their boss by telling him about the miracles that Jesus was doing. He requested a private audience with Jesus, but the Master refused the man no one said no to. The royal ruler didn't take the refusal lightly and put a hit out on Jesus, but his soldiers could never find the Miracle Worker.

One day a surprise came to Herod from Pontius Pilate. His army came to the king with a request. The governor was asking him to question Jesus. Antipas was delighted.

*He has recognized my keen insight and astute leadership qualities at last. I'm gonna get to see a magic show after all.*

Herod greeted the man who'd come to save him in a sauced stupor. In slurred speech he boomed, "Finally we meet. I've heard so much about your magic powers, do a miracle for me."

Jesus was silent.

"Didn't you hear me? I said do some sorcery, now you miserable little Jew!"

The Savior remained quiet. It enraged the king, and he threw a temper tantrum. He ranted to his soldiers.

"No one disobeys my orders. He's touched in the head. Why is Pilate sending me a lunatic? Do you see why I can't associate with common people–they're too stupid for someone as sharp as me."

He screamed at Jesus, "You crazy son of a viper! I'll teach you what I do to people who defy me!

Herod's soldiers had a field day whipping and pounding on Jesus. The Tetrarch sent him back to Pilate. "He's umpatz! I couldn't get anything out of him. I'm not gonna condemn him and cause riots among the Jews. Thanks for your confidence in my leadership, but I'll leave his judgment to you."

A merciful God sent his best to Herod to try to save him from himself and his many evil ways. But the Almighty would not override the king's willful disobedience and rejection of his prophets. The day of judgment finally arrived for the sadistic ruler. Shortly after he rejected the Son of God, the rebellious leader was giving a pompous speech. As he was speaking his stomach burst open with worms exploding everywhere.

A fit reward for an unfit ruler.

> *"But the fearful, and unbelieving, and the abominable, and murderers, and whoremongers, and sorcerers, and idolaters, and all liars, shall have their part in the lake which burns with fire and brimstone; which is the second death."*
>
> *Revelation 21:7-8*

Many physicians and Bible scholars believe Herod died of syphilis. You can read about Herod's final moments in Acts 13.

## Chapter 21

# The Truly Good Fella

*"Today I saw a slave become more powerful than the Emperor of Rome."*

*-The Gladiator*

URSING, screaming, and hysterical weeping resounded through the crowded streets. In the middle of the chaos was the Sanhedrin, Jews from several nations, and followers of the Nazarene. Many travelers had come from abroad to celebrate the Passover. It looked like anything but a celebration. The pilgrims and locals were being shoved out of the way by Roman soldiers.

"Get outta the way. Mind your own business. Clear these streets or you'll be next," the Centurion shouted.

"Papa what's happening? Why are all these people acting like this?" asked young Rufus, his trembling voice full of fear.

"I don't know, son, but you and your brother Alexander need to get up against the walls so you don't get crushed or clubbed."

Simon's massive frame and dark skin made him stand out in the crowd. As he was trying to shield his two sons from the frenzied multitude, he felt a sharp kick in his ribs.

"*Mulyam,* pick up this cross!" demanded a soldier riding a horse. "Be quick about it or I'll rearrange your face."

The black man knew he had no choice. No one argued with the Romans and lived to talk about it.

*Where are they taking me and how far will I have to go?* He quickly shouted to his older son, "Alexander, follow me and hold onto your brother. Don't let Rufus out of your sight!"

As the anxious father swiftly bent to pick up the cross, he saw him. A man saturated in blood staggered behind the soldier. Chunks of his beard were missing. Large thorns were sticking out of his head. His shredded flesh exposed bones and deep wounds. A crimson path trailed the footsteps of the man.

*Look at this poor man. How can anyone still be alive after losing so much blood? What is his crime? I wish I could do more for him.*

As the African lifted the immense cross, deep, thick splinters of wood gauged open his back. He silently shouldered the heavy burden. His own sweat and blood mingled with that of the condemned man. Simon also stumbled as he struggled to drag the cross up a hill. The area was called Golgotha, which means, "Place of the Skull."

Finally the Centurion yelled, "Leave it there, *Mulyam!*"

Simon dropped his heavy load and worriedly scanned the vast crowd for his two sons. After a panic-stricken period of time, he found them and hugged the two tightly to his own blood-soaked chest. The African's big, ripped open arms shook as he squeezed his children. His voice broke while speaking to them. "I'm so sorry you boys had to experience this."

They were both sobbing and trembling. *Thank You, Father they're okay.*

The overwrought father tried to block the view of Rufus and Alexander as the Romans drove the nine inch nails through the hands and feet of the one they called Jesus. The mass of people made it impossible for the father and his sons to push through away from the horrific scene. As difficult as it was to remain, Simon was captivated by the crowds and their testimonies of miracles and healings.

*I can't believe the contrast! The religious organized crime leaders are actually rejoicing at this man's beating and torture. Who would want to serve the God they say they represent? Yet, the common Jews worship him as the Messiah. Why would all these people lie about the miracles and risk death? I've never seen someone dying such an agonizing death and yet be so caring and loving. They say he's the Son of God. I believe it.*

Simon returned to his home country several days later, unaware of the magnitude of his deed. It was not an Italian, a Jew, or even a disciple that God, the Father called upon that day. The Lord summoned an African to demonstrate what true strength of character is. The courageous foreigner didn't complain. He didn't run from the pain or hardship of lifting someone else's back-breaking load. God used a compassionate, dark-skinned man to help his Son carry a weight that was more than he could bear.

The black man's selfless display of honor was greatly rewarded by his heavenly Father in years to come. Simon's sons became pillars in the early church. They were both known to Mark, writer of one of the four gospels. The apostle Paul also acknowledged and spoke highly of Rufus in the book of Romans. Thousands of years after the fact, the Lord still has the world reading about the heroic act of the father of Rufus and Alexander, proving God is not a respecter of race or color. He honors faith and integrity wherever it is found.

*God is not unjust; He will not forget your work and the love you have shown him as you have helped his people and continue to help them.*
*Hebrews 6:10*

CHAPTER 22

# The Thief Who Got Pinched

*"There's two endings for a guy like me: dead or in the can."*
*-Tony Soprano*

T HE pain made his head spin as they hoisted him up. Sights and sounds were a blur. The thief drifted in and out of unconsciousness, but the unrelenting punishment to his body always brought him back around. He felt like his hands were going to be ripped from his wrists by the nails that had been driven through them. His feet burned and stung from the nine inch nails that had been hammered into them.

He had received some bad beat-downs in his day, but none compared to being hung on a cross. The deep splinters from the wood were tearing apart his flesh. His entire body was on fire screaming with pain. The intensity of what he was feeling made him meaner than he already was.

Slowly he began to distinguish the sounds around him. He could tell he was surrounded by a noisy, huge crowd. The soldiers were cursing at him and whoever else they had just crucified. But there was an argument going on. He could hear the Jewish Sanhedrin hissing,

"Remove that. He's not our King. He's the only one who says

that. He's a liar and a thief. He's a magician. He was trying to incite riots among the people. He calls himself the Son of God. He's been condemned by your government. Don't let this liar die with that title over his head."

The Roman leg-breaker shot a fed-up look at his *paesano*. "Are these people a piece of work or what?"

The head Centurion addressed the Chief Priest whose face was as purple as the garment he wore. "It says King of the Jews. This is what Pontius Pilate ordered. I run this operation. Nobody but Pilate tells me what to do. Ya got problems with it, take it up with my boss. This is the way it's gonna stay, *cappish*? Don't argue with me. I'm in a bad mood. I wouldn't mind bustin' a few more heads today."

The condemned crook couldn't believe his ears. *I hate the religious syndicate even more than I hate the Romans. Here I am dying and these bloodsuckers gotta show up. I'll meet 'em in hell one day, but until then, why do they care about a convicted con?*

The thief's distorted vision was starting to clear. He was able to make out two men on crosses next to him. He recognized the other man crucified furthest from him. They were never *goombas* but they were both in the same racket. He was swearing loudly and mocking the one they said was the King of the Jews.

"I'm a Jew, but I ain't ever called myself a king. Who does Mister high and mighty think he is? Hey magician, do some magic tricks and get us outta here. You're a joke. I'm getting pleasure thinkin' about how they beat you like an animal."

When the other thief heard that this man in the middle of them had called himself the Son of God, he became infuriated. He joined the other fuming felon.

"You been running a religious racket? I know all about your kind. You're the worst. At least I admit to being a thief, but I never used the sacred scam. Good you scum, you got pinched. I'm glad they finally caught one of you phony preachers. Now you're getting what you and all of your kind deserve."

The man in between the two thieves didn't answer back. The religious organized crime leaders continued to mock and scorn the man.

Jesus was the man in the middle. His followers were present also. The condemned con recognized Mary the prostitute. She was dressed like a decent woman now. She was weeping for the one she called Master.

She testified to the ones around her, "He changed my life. He is a holy man. He only does good. The only thing he is guilty of is kindness and love."

The widow was tearfully telling those around her, "My son died. Jesus brought him back to life. I beg you to save my Savior's life."

Another cried out, "I was blind now I see. No one who is evil could do this."

On and on they testified, people who maintained that he had healed them and truly did work miracles.

The thief on the right side of the one they called the Son of God observed him. He and the crook on the opposite side were knocked around before they were crucified. But you wouldn't even know the one between them was a man. He was a mass of blood and shredded skin. His bones stuck out. On his head was a circle of thorns. Parts of his beard had been yanked out. This guy was beat worse than anyone he'd ever seen, yet he was dying without complaint.

It was a sweltering day. The thief on the right of Jesus felt his skin scorching. His thirst was unquenchable. He was gasping for every breathe he took. He had no more strength to ridicule. Then he heard the one called Jesus speak.

"Father, forgive them. They don't know what they are doing."

The con on the right was incredulous. *At the very last minutes of his life, he is still reaching out to the hateful. Who is he talking about? The Roman leg-breakers are gambling for his robe. The temple mobsters are having a party over his death. Why is he freakin' forgiving any of them?*

Jesus gasped as he spoke to some people below the cross. Compassion and love saturated his words.

"John, take my Mama home with you. From this day forward, she will be your mother. Mama, from now on John is the son who will take care of you."

The thief on the right thought about his own mother. He was grateful his mother was no longer alive to witness his crucifixion. The mother of Jesus was so beside herself with grief she was having trouble breathing. It was almost as if she was trying to breath for her son. She had to be held up by those around her.

So many people were crying for Jesus. His followers were risking their lives by being present at his crucifixion, yet they remained.

They were Jews. They knew the religious syndicate would now count them as enemies. They could face the same fate as the one they called Healer, yet they stood not caring what judgment might follow.

*Why are they endangering themselves? How can this man be thinking about others when he is in such a horrible state? Only someone from heaven can act like this man. God must surely have given him this power.*

All at once the thief knew. He was in the presence of perfect love. He felt the acceptance and forgiveness of Jesus. The Master did not condemn him. Although he was experiencing mind-blowing pain, the crook on the right addressed the other criminal. He spoke in whispered, halting speech.

"We deserve to die for what we have done. We are guilty. But this man hasn't hurt anybody. He has given mercy and prayed for the ones who set him up. He's in so much more pain than we are, but he is still showing such incredible love. There is no hate in him, even for the men who did this to him. He's a stand-up guy."

The love of Jesus had triumphed over evil. The thief on the right of Jesus struggled for air. Even though he couldn't see the face of the Master because it was so full of blood, he called on him.

"Jesus, I know you're not a false prophet or magician. I believe you are the Son of God. Forgive me for the life I've lived. I know I was wrong. Have mercy on me. Remember me when you come into your kingdom."

Jesus extended one last act of kindness before he died.

"You are forgiven. Your sins will not be held against you. Fear not. This day you'll be with me in heaven."

The Son of God spoke his final words. "It is finished."

The thick curtain in the temple was ripped by God from top to bottom. Men and women would no longer be separated from him by a curtain or corrupt temple mobsters.

It was still daylight, but the sky went black. God's anger resonated throughout the earth. The entire world seemed to shudder. The Son of God had died.

Later on that day, the Roman soldiers came to break the legs of the two thieves to hasten their death. Both crooks were hard-core criminals. The two of them had derided and cursed Jesus and everyone else present. Only one would ask for mercy.

God passed over most of the religious leaders that claimed to know him that day. Instead, He embraced a repentant felon. The Father accepted Jesus as the Passover Lamb for the sins of a fallen world. The angels rejoiced. All who would acknowledge his Son, Jesus and repent would be saved. The Father and His perfect Son had planned it that way from the beginning. The thief on the right hand of Jesus had started the morning hating the world and everybody in it. He died a man condemned by people, but found not guilty by God.

*"Then I acknowledged my sin to you and did not cover up my iniquity.*
*' I said, I will confess my transgressions to the Lord'-and you forgave*
*the guilt of my sins. "*

*Psalm 32:5*

# The Stand-Up Guy

*The devils that are not in hell are in Rome.*

-*Italian proverb*

H E had been beaten and tortured beyond what any human being could endure, yet he endured. He wasn't guilty, but he didn't try to defend himself. Jesus knew things that could bring every crime family down, but he didn't rat them out. He had forgiven all his accusers and tormentors. He held no bitterness in his heart. His last assignment before he died was completed. He had demonstrated the Father's love to a convicted felon. Jesus would see the repentant thief in heaven.

He took the fall for crimes he didn't carry out, for sins he didn't commit. But the one question his mother, his disciples, his enemies, and the religious syndicate wanted to know was, *why?*

The Healer knew the end from the beginning.

*"Wherefore seeing we also are compassed about with so great a cloud of witnesses, let us lay aside every weight, and the sin which doth so easily beset us, and let us run with patience, the race that is set before us. Looking unto Jesus the author and finisher of our faith; who for the joy that was set before him endured the cross, despising the shame and is set down at the right hand of the throne of God. For*

*consider him that endureth such contradiction against himself, lest ye*
*be wearied and faint in your minds. "*

*Hebrews 12: 1-3*

When he was being beaten and tortured for something he was not guilty of–He stood. When the accusations raged–He stood. When they beat him with their fists and yanked out his beard and whipped him–He stood.

On the cross, Jesus saw the people he was dying for, but God granted him the privilege of seeing all who would come later. He saw the grief-stricken parents of a deceased child. He took their pain. He saw the drug addicts with the needles in their arms. He felt their agony. He bore it on Calvary.

Jesus saw thousands of years ahead in time. He saw the present-day mob. He witnessed the tormented individuals who thought there was no way out. He became their Way. He caught sight of the loneliness of the shut-ins, the elderly, the rejected, the betrayed, and he took their cruel isolation into himself. He stood in their place.

He stood for every criminal: all the self-righteous, every deceived person, and all who were tormented by disease. He received their sin and sickness upon himself. He looked across the ages.

To the abused woman, He said, "I'm giving up my life so that you don't have to give up yours."

To all good fellas, felons, alcoholics, and addicts of every kind, He said, "I'm dying in your place. Be free."

To the slaves of sex sin, adultery, and perversion of all types, He said, "I'm being condemned in your place, go and sin no more."

To the religious leaders and hypocrites, who pretended to live holy lives but didn't know him or the Father, He said, "Behold I stand at the door, and knock: if any man hears my voice, and opens the door, I will come in to him, and will sup with him, and he with me."

God who became man, voluntarily signed up for this assignment. He would lay aside his deity and become a man. He was totally dependent on the Holy Spirit to administer miracles and healings. He knew he would feel pain, disease, and condemnation for the first time ever. He would leave the perfection and beauty of heaven to come to a lost and dying world. He was aware that the only way to bring sinful man to heaven was to become cursed and condemned in humanity's place. He did it. He was the Stand-Up Guy.

All of heaven applauded as the Stand-Up Guy single-handedly took on the entirety of hell's power. The combined demonic force of every fallen angel was no match for the Deliverer. When Satan and all his demons came to torture him, they taunted him saying,

"You belong to us now. You are damned. You are ours for all eternity. So many sins were found in you that it will take us forever to punish you for your transgressions."

Hell quaked as Jesus confronted dethroned Lucifer and his evil cohorts. The phrase, "No Fear" did not originate with the clothing line. It originated with Jesus, the Conqueror of Sin. When Satan said, "You fell or you wouldn't be here."

Jesus answered him with God-given boldness and fearless strength,

"I'm still standing, and I'm not going down. You tried to make me fall, but you failed. I died once for every man for all eternity. Your stranglehold on mankind is over. I'm here in the place of every sinner. I received their judgment. I exchanged their sin for my righteousness. For every one of them who will call on my name, God will see them as not guilty. I took their punishment."

The Savior's heroic act made a way for all humanity to enter heaven. Jesus took the keys of hell and death that day. The greatest Stand-Up Guy of all time had triumphed over evil and temptation of every kind.

His followers rejoiced on the third day when they realized the Savior they had committed their lives to was no longer dead, but alive. They understood that Jesus had died in their place. Calvary wasn't the end; it was a beginning. The cruel cross was not a place of defeat, but of power and victory. Jesus had triumphed and won.

No longer would men and women have to pay to have their prayers answered. Jesus had instructed them, "Whatever you desire, in line with my Word and will, ask the Father in my name and He will give it to you."

The Savior had told them, "It's better for you that I go away. If I don't go the Comforter, Helper, Advocate will not come. But when I go, I will send him to you. You'll never be alone because he will never leave you nor forsake you. He will give you power to resist and overcome all evil, as I have done."

They knew their Savior was Lord over all adversity. Because of it they could live without seeing him on the earth.

Satan and his evil cohorts did not understand that God is light and in Him is no darkness at all. The regions of hell trembled as the Father spoke.

*"See, my Servant shall prosper; he shall be highly exalted. Yet many shall be amazed when they see him-yes, even far-off nations and their kings; they shall stand dumbfounded, speechless in his presence. For they shall see and understand what they had not been told before. They shall see my Servant beaten and bloodied, so disfigured one would scarcely know it was a person standing there. So shall he cleanse many nations.*

*"But, oh, how few believe it! Who will listen? To whom will God reveal his saving power? In God's eyes he was like a tender green shoot, sprouting from a root in dry and sterile ground. But in our*

*eyes there was no attractiveness at all, nothing to make us want him. We despised him and rejected him-a man of sorrows, acquainted with bitterest grief. We turned our back on him and looked the other way when he went by. He was despised and we didn't care.*

*"Yet it was our grief he bore, our sorrows that weighed him down. And we thought his troubles were a punishment from God, for his own sins! But he was wounded and bruised for our sins. He was beaten that we might have peace; he was lashed-and we were healed! We-every one of us-have strayed away like sheep! We, who left God's paths to follow our own. Yet God laid on him the guilt and sins of every one of us!"*

*Isaiah 52: 13-15; 53:1-6*

# Author's Note

No matter what situation or problem you are facing, no matter how bad things may look, The Stand-Up Guy will make a way where there seems to be no way. Having lived a life of many gut-wrenching circumstances, challenges, heartbreaks, and pits so dark and deep, I thought I'd never experience joy again, I can tell you the greatest Stand-Up Guy of all time, Jesus, was there for me through it all. He did it for me and he'll do it for you. May God bless you in your journey.

For additional materials
or speaking engagements contact:

Susan Eaves
P.O. Box 7
Osprey, Fl. 34229

GoodFellasoftheBible.com

# Good Fellas' Publishing Order Form

Please send me ____ copies of *Good Fellas of the Bible* @ $15 per book plus shipping and handling.

Please send me ____ copies of *The I Am Book (A Compilation of scriptures on God's Character and who we are in Him)*, @ $15 per book plus shipping and handling. Group discounts available.

Please make checks payable to: Good Fellas Publishing. Prices subject to change. Shipping and handling: $4.95 per book.

TOTAL ENCLOSED: $_____

Name _____

Address _____

City _____

State / Zip _____

Please send to: Good Fellas Publishing, P. O. Box 7, Osprey, FL 34229.

www.GoodFellasoftheBible.com

# Good Fellas' Publishing Order Form

Please send me _____ copies of *Good Fellas of the Bible*
@ $15 per book plus shipping and handling.

Please send me _____ copies of *The I Am Book (A Compilation
of scriptures on God's Character and who we are in Him)*,
@ $15 per book plus shipping and handling. Group
discounts available.

Please make checks payable to: Good Fellas Publishing.
Prices subject to change. Shipping and handling: $4.95 per
book.


TOTAL ENCLOSED: $_____

Name _____

Address _____

City _____

State / Zip _____


Please send to: Good Fellas Publishing,
P. O. Box 7, Osprey, FL 34229.

www.GoodFellasoftheBible.com